"Take me to the police."

"Take the exit," I say loudly. "Take me to the police."

They stop arguing.

We don't get into the exit lane.

"The exit!" I practically shout. "Get over."

They keep looking ahead.

"What are you doing? Get over! Please, please get over." I grab the old man's shoulder and shake. He just drives. They're not taking me to the police. Oh, they're not taking me to the police. Where are they taking me?

I scream as we pass the exit. I scream and scream.

★ "Nightmarish scenes . . . a suspenseful reading experience."
—*SLJ*, starred review

"Jackie's situation is highly compelling. . . . Readers are sufficiently grabbed by Jackie's ingenuous voice and her remarkable predicament." —*Kirkus Reviews*

A BANK STREET COLLEGE BEST CHILDREN'S BOOK OF THE YEAR
A WILLIAM ALLEN WHITE AWARD NOMINEE

three days

three days

DONNA JO NAPOLI

PUFFIN BOOKS

Thanks to my family, and Lina Mirarchi, Rosaria Munson, Richard Tchen, and Celeste McLaughlin's fifth-grade class at the Wallingford-Swarthmore School in spring 2000, and a special thank you to my editor, Lucia Monfried.

PUFFIN BOOKS
Published by Penguin Group,
Penguin Young Readers Group,
345 Hudson Street, New York, New York 10014, U.S.A.
Penguin Books Ltd, 80 Strand, London WC2R ORL, England
Penguin Books Australia Ltd, Ringwood, Victoria, Australia
Penguin Books Canada Ltd, 10 Alcorn Avenue, Toronto, Ontario, Canada M4V 3B2
Penguin Books (N.Z.) Ltd, 182-190 Wairau Road, Auckland 10, New Zealand

First published in the United States of America by Dutton Children's Books, a division of
Penguin Putnam Books for Young Readers, 2001
Published by Puffin Books, a division of Penguin Young Readers Group, 2003

1 3 5 7 9 10 8 6 4 2

THE LIBRARY OF CONGRESS HAS CATALOGED THE DUTTON EDITION AS FOLLOWS:
Napoli, Donna Jo, date.
Three Days / by Donna Jo Napoli.—1st ed.
p.   cm.
Summary: When her father suddenly dies while on a business trip, leaving her alone on an Italian highway, eleven-year-old Jackie worries what will happen when she is picked up by two men with unknown motives.
ISBN: 0-525-46790-4 (hc)
[1. Kidnapping—Fiction.   2. Italy—Fiction.]   I. Title.
PZ7.N15 Th 2001   [Fic]—dc21   2001028535

Puffin Books ISBN 0-14-250025-9

Printed in the United States of America

For Nick—thank you

three days

①

"Try some?" Daddy pushes the bowl toward me. Actually, it isn't really a bowl. It's sort of a goblet, like in the old days. Lots of things here are old. Like the buildings. And the paintings.

The sides of the goblet are bumpy with clusters of glass grapes. It's beautiful. Elegant. I feel like I'm a princess or something, living long ago. Like I feel when I crawl into the big bed in our hotel room. It's so high that I have to climb.

I sniff the golden cream. The sharp scent surprises me. I dip in the very tip of my spoon. Most of the time when I try new foods here I like them. But not this time. "It's okay." I push the goblet back toward Daddy.

Daddy laughs. "Zabaglione is a real treat. My favorite dessert. But I was afraid you might not like it, so

I'm glad I ordered only one. Would you like something else?"

"Ice cream. One scoop of chocolate. No, two."

Daddy laughs again. "That's my girl. Italian ice cream is the best in the world." He calls over the waiter.

A minute later I'm eating the creamiest, darkest chocolate ice cream I've ever had.

"Good, huh?" Daddy finishes off his dessert and watches me finish mine. "We need to hit the road and get you in bed." He pays the bill.

I hurry to the bathroom. It's a long drive back to our hotel. Over an hour. And there isn't really anyplace to stop along the way. I learned that the other day, when I made the mistake of drinking two Cokes before getting into the car.

Daddy's waiting for me by the door when I come out. I take his hand. In America I'd never do that. I'm eleven, after all. But here in Italy I've seen girls older than me take their father's hand. Teenagers. It's weird, but in lots of ways I've been acting younger this trip. I feel like a little kid. Maybe because I can't speak to anyone but Daddy—I don't speak Italian. And because things are different here. Little things, but so many of them. It's fun to notice all the little things. And it's fun to pretend I'm Italian—an Italian girl taking her Italian daddy's hand.

I love holding hands with Daddy. He has big hands.

Daddy squeezes my hand tenderly. He goes out of his way to thank the waiter before we leave. In America we never do that, either. But Daddy says that's the way it's done here. If you don't stop and talk to people, they think you're rude.

I like that, too. I like everything about being here.

The activity outside on the sidewalk makes me happy. At home the sidewalks are never this busy, even in the middle of the day. Now it feels almost like a party.

We drive slowly through the streets of Rome, with the windows up and the air-conditioning on.

"I don't suppose you'd like these?" Daddy drops something in my lap.

It's a miniature box of those candies I love—Baci. They're chocolate mixed with some kind of nut, and each of them is wrapped in a piece of shiny silver foil with teeny blue stars. I giggle and eat all three. Daddy does things like that; he gives little surprises all the time. "They were yummy. Thank you."

Daddy glances over quickly and smiles. Then his eyes are back on the road. He's a good driver. Mamma always says that. "In America those candies come with little sayings in them."

"What do you mean?" I ask. "Like in fortune cookies?"

"Sort of. But the sayings are always about love. *Baci* means 'kisses.' "

"Like Hershey's." Then I laugh. "But a zillion times better."

Daddy laughs, too. "You've become a Baci piggy." He shifts gears as he changes lanes and speeds up. I expect him to say something about Italian cars and how much he enjoys driving this one. He says things like that just about every time we get on the road. He gives a contented little hum. "We can get Baci in America when we go back. I can buy them for you year round."

"Thanks." I put the empty candy box on the floor, reminding myself to throw it in the trash when we get back to the hotel.

I wiggle back in the seat till I'm comfortable, then I smooth my dress over my knees. At home I wear dresses only to church and to parties. But Daddy likes me to put them on when we're spending the day with one of the men he does business with. Like we did today. This dress has big flowers printed all over it, and in the center of each flower there's a thick black knot of thread, like in a black-eyed Susan. I run the tip of my index finger in a circle over one of the knots on my belly.

"Traffic is heavy," Daddy says almost to himself.

"It's always this way. Don't worry. We'll be back at the hotel soon."

"We've been here less than two weeks and already you know all about it, huh? That's my smart girl." Daddy turns his head again to give me another smile. Then he switches on the radio. "It's late." He belches and rubs his left arm. "You can fall asleep if you want, Jackie. I'll wake you when we get there."

"I'm not sleepy." And, anyway, I think, I don't like to fall asleep in cars. It means that I'll feel all confused when Daddy wakes me up to go into the hotel. Plus, if I fall asleep, I'll probably slump over and wrinkle my dress. And this is a pretty dress. We bought it here. My shoes are new, too. They're patent leather, and they have a strap that goes across the front and buckles. No one at home has even seen them yet.

Thinking like this makes me miss home. I miss my dog, Jersey. And my best friend, Noëlle. But, most of all, I miss Mamma. This is the first time I've ever been away from her for more than an overnight, except to go to Grandma and Grandpa's for a long weekend. Daddy goes on business trips all around America and Europe often. A few times every year. And Mamma and I keep each other company. But this time Daddy said I should come with him. It's a longer trip than usual—three whole weeks. He said he'd get lonely. And it's summertime, so I'm not missing school. Plus Mamma said it would be good for me in lots of ways.

It's fun, of course. I mean, anything with Daddy is fun. He's always asking me what I want. And he lets me try new things. When a waiter asked if I wanted wine, Daddy just lifted his eyebrows at me—it was my choice. I didn't want any. But I could have had it. That's what matters. And every time he hears of some beautiful statue or fountain or anything, he takes me to see it. Daddy wants me to enjoy this trip. But right now I suddenly feel like I'm ready to go home. I wish we were leaving tomorrow.

My eyes feel heavy. The car does that. And Daddy's right: at home I'd have been in bed by now. People eat dinner really late here. I blink, to clear my head.

When we got in the car, it was still twilight, but it got dark in an instant. Daddy's driving fast now. We're on the highway. Our hotel is in a small town south of Rome. Daddy doesn't like to stay in cities. He says people in cities are too rushed. People in small towns take the time to get to know you a little. Especially in the south. Daddy says the people in the south are the friendliest. He says the farther south you go, the poorer the people get, but the friendlier, too. And it must be true, because our hotel owner has a drink with Daddy every night, and they talk and laugh. The day after we arrived he took us on a walk through the vineyards down the road from the hotel. He told us about everything. I had no idea what he was saying, because his accent in English is so heavy. I had a good time anyway, because we stopped at a small house where they had a funny little wooden shed full of baby rabbits and their mothers. The woman who owned the rabbits put a bundle of straw in the middle of the shed, and I got to sit on it with baby rabbits hopping all over me. They were softer than I'd ever imagined anything could be.

"Could we visit the rabbits again?" I ask.

Daddy makes a strange cough and rubs his left arm harder than he did before.

"The baby rabbits," I say, looking at him. "Can we go see them again?"

Daddy's mouth is open as he looks at me. He gags.

"Daddy? Daddy, are you all right?"

His eyes are huge. He seems almost frightened. His hands are tight on the steering wheel, tight and rigid, like the rest of him. He makes a series of gasps and pulls the car over to the side of the highway. We're still going fast, and the car bounces over the rough ground.

"Daddy!" I'm scared now. I squeeze my hands together. "Daddy, what's the matter? What are you doing?"

The car comes to a stop and the motor dies with a lurch. Daddy grabs the keys and slumps over the steering wheel.

"Why are we stopping? Are you okay?" I shake his arm. "Daddy?"

He doesn't answer.

I unbuckle my seat belt and kneel on my seat so I can get a better grip on him. I pull his arm. He falls sideways across the gear stick between the seats. The keys fall from his right hand.

Everything is wrong.

I touch his face. His eyes are open, but they don't move. This can't be happening. Horrible things like this don't just happen. He was fine a moment ago. No, no, no.

"Daddy," I'm screaming, "Daddy, Daddy."

②

Help!" I wave my arms over my head and try to flag down a car. "Please, help!" I shout. Someone has to stop fast. Daddy needs help right now.

The cars zoom past.

I look back at the car behind me, at Daddy. Only one shoulder of his shows, and just barely. He hasn't moved. But it's only been a couple of minutes. It couldn't be more than that. He'll be okay.

As long as someone stops and helps us.

I wish I knew how to say "help" in Italian.

The night air is black and there are no streetlights. People can see the car, because I left my door open, so the inside overhead light is on. But they probably don't see me standing out here behind the car. The headlights of the car went out when the motor turned off. If I stood in the headlights, people would see me. I have to turn the motor back on.

I rush back to my side of the car, crawl into the floor space in front of my seat, and reach my arm across to the floor space under Daddy's legs. My fingers find the keys right away.

Hurry. I've got to hurry.

I've never turned on a car before, but it can't be hard. There are two keys. The first one fits. I turn it. The motor starts and the car jerks forward and dies. I try the other key. It won't go in. I jam the first one back in and try again. The car jerks forward and dies.

There's got to be another way to get the lights on.

The pullout button for the lights in our car at home is on the left side of the driver. Maybe it's the same in this car. I could kneel on my seat and reach across Daddy. But I don't want to press on him—I don't want to risk hurting him.

I get out and run around the car and go to open Daddy's door. It's locked.

A car passes, then slows down. Its brake lights shine red.

"Help!" I shout, running after it, waving my hands in front of me like a maniac. "Hurry!"

The car goes on.

How could they? I know they saw me. I was smack

up against the car when they slowed down, so I showed in the little overhead light.

I run back to my side of the car and reach through the front to unlock my backseat door. Then I get in the back and lean over from behind Daddy, feeling around on the dashboard for the lights. The way he's slumped over, I don't even have to touch him to do it, so I know I'm not disturbing him. "It'll be okay, Daddy," I say. "Someone's going to stop." I pull a knob. The headlights come on.

I race back outside and stand in the headlights and wave my arms and shout.

The next cars are fast. The swirl of wind as they pass pushes me back a few steps. Someone has to stop. Anyone can see we're in trouble—they have to stop.

I wave my arms over my head as high as I can. I jump in place. "Help." I'm breathing so hard, the word barely comes out. No one could ever hear me, even shouting. The traffic noise is loud, and their windows are up anyway.

The horn. They'd hear the horn. I get in the backseat of the car again and reach over Daddy and press on the horn. Nothing. Our car horn at home works when the car is off—why doesn't this stupid horn work? I bang my fist on the horn. Nothing.

I jump out and try to flag down traffic again. But no one stops.

How long has it been?

I'm shouting and jumping and waving and no one's stopping.

And Daddy's all alone in the car. How long has it been? I can't be sure. The only sure thing is that Daddy needs help quick. I don't know how to help him, I don't know what to do, I don't know anything. But I've got to try.

I get in the car and turn Daddy's head to face me. I blow in his mouth, over and over. I push his shoulder up so I can reach his chest, and I pound on his heart.

He's totally limp. I think he's not breathing.

Don't think. Don't think like that.

I count inside my head as I blow in his mouth. I count as I pound on his heart. When I reach a thousand, I stop. This isn't working.

And maybe my pounding hurts him.

I get out of the car and climb into the backseat. This way I can pat Daddy's face from behind without pressing on his chest or shoulders. I straddle the hump on the floor in the middle of the backseat and gently rub his cheek. "Wake up, Daddy. Please." I rub harder. "Don't do this. Please, please don't do this, Daddy." My hands slap on his soft skin. He won't wake.

Time is passing, and Daddy won't wake.

I fight the urge to cry. I have to figure out what to do.

But I won't leave Daddy alone anymore. He might be in a coma. And people in a coma can hear. That's what they say. I know people say that.

Okay, I'll stay in the car and wave my hands at the passing cars. People will see me because I left the front door open, so the little overhead light is on. And they'll know we're in trouble because the headlights are on.

"Don't be afraid, Daddy. Someone will stop soon. I'll sing to you." I start with the songs he likes to sing, James Taylor hits. We sing them together in the car at home all the time. I'm waving my hands frantically over my head as I go through every James Taylor song I know, twice. Three times. I sing anything that comes to mind. Songs I learned in school. That's weird, because I don't even like a lot of them. But they're in my head. And now I sing Christmas songs. So many Christmas songs. My throat gets hoarse because I have to sing loud to be heard over the noise of the highway.

Light shines through the rear window. I look back. A car has pulled up behind us. Oh, yes, finally. I quick pull on the back-door handle and leap out. It's a white beat-up car with two men in the front. They're talking to each other—arguing, I think. Suddenly they take off.

I run after them, my hands over my head. "Stop!" I know they can hear me—their windows are down.

They're gone.

Gone.

What's the matter with everyone?

"Stop!" I scream at no one.

The swoosh of wind from a passing truck knocks me off my feet and sucks me onto the road. I jump up and scramble back to the shoulder, farther back than before. My knees and shins are scraped. Blood thumps in my temples and chest. If a car had come along just then, I'd have been crushed.

I run back to the car and jump into the back. "It's okay, Daddy. We'll be all right." I work hard to keep the shrill of panic out of my voice, just in case Daddy's really listening. He shouldn't be scared. I have to sing. Just sing and sing and sing. The same songs, again and again. Sing and wave my arms.

After a while it feels like I've been singing forever.

The overhead light gradually dims and goes out. So do the headlights.

How long has it been? How long does a car battery take to die?

We're in total dark.

I hush and lock my backseat door instinctively. That was silly; there's no one here. No one but Daddy and me. Plus my front door is still standing open. I don't close it, though. I should, but I don't. Mamma says I'm always practical. It isn't practical to leave one door open. But I can't reach the handle to close it from the inside without climbing over the seat, and I don't want to jostle Daddy.

The only other choice is to get out of the car and close the door, but I don't want to get out of the car in the dark.

I shiver in the heat.

The back of the car smells stale.

My arms ache from all that waving I did. But there's no point in waving anymore. No one can see me without the overhead light.

I sing again. My songs seem louder in the dark. That's one good thing, at least. I sway as I sing.

It's amazingly hot. But I want the doors closed. I'm shaking all over.

Slowly, though, the shakes stop. I brush Daddy's hair back in place with my hands. I've got to do something. "Someone's going to stop soon, Daddy." I breathe shallow in the heat. "I'll get out again and flag down a car. It'll work this time," I say. "I'm not really afraid of the trucks. I'll just run way back onto the shoulder when I see a big truck coming."

I get out of the car and stand behind it and wave my

arms and shout. But I know this isn't going to work. It didn't work when the lights were on; it won't work now.

I get back into the car, into the front seat now. I smooth Daddy's cheek. He's warm to the touch, but not hot. Only warm, on this hot, hot night. I put my hands on my own cheeks. They're slick with sweat.

And there's something else about Daddy's cheek now. The skin has changed texture. It's not soft anymore.

No. No and no and no.

My head fills with noise, like the buzz of a chain saw in the fall back home. Everything seems slow. Even the passing cars. Slow motion.

I fold my hands in my lap. My tongue feels huge within my mouth. I can't move it. I can't move anything. The air inside the car is thick and stuffy. I can hardly breathe.

I force myself to press the window button. It doesn't work. Of course.

I open the glove compartment and take out the stuffed animal that Daddy's business friend gave me this morning. It's a striped cat. I don't play much with stuffed animals anymore. I wind its long tail around my arm.

I shouldn't have come on this trip. Oh, but if I hadn't, Daddy would have been alone when this happened.

I want Mamma.

Numbers fill my head, emergency numbers: 320-555-2149. My phone number, with the area code. I don't know how to dial it from Italy. There are extra numbers that go on at the beginning. Daddy told me, but I didn't learn them by heart, because Daddy said that in an emergency I can pick up a phone and speak slowly and loudly in English and say I want this number in the United States. Not America. I'm supposed to say "The United States," like that.

A phone. I don't know where there's a phone.

"Daddy." I put my cheek against the top of his head. I hold his hand. It's cooler now—just a little bit—but I can feel it. And the fingers are stiff. I put both my hands around Daddy's hand and rub it softly to warm it up.

I close my eyes.

Something's different. My eyelids pop open and I look out on the cars ahead of us on the road—at their taillights. Time has snapped back to normal. Everyone's going so fast. And there's light again. Light coming into the car from behind.

Before I can even jump out, my door opens. A man speaks to me in Italian.

Oh, thank you, God. All my pent-up tears come gushing out. "Help. Call an ambulance."

The man leans all the way across me, across Daddy,

and unlocks Daddy's door. Another man, an old man, opens Daddy's door from outside. He feels Daddy's wrist.

"He just collapsed," I say, though I'm crying so hard now, my talk comes out ragged. "Call an ambulance. Hurry."

Now the old man's going through Daddy's sportscoat pockets. He looks at Daddy's passport. Then at mine.

The young man grabs me by the hand and rushes me to their car. I don't want to leave Daddy all alone. But I don't know what else to do. I don't know anything. The man jerks his front seat forward. I climb into the backseat. He gets in the front. The old man jumps in the driver's seat.

The car takes off fast. We're going to the hospital. I look out the back window. Our car is out of sight almost immediately.

Daddy's gone.

The old man hands my toy cat to the young man, who turns and hands it to me, speaking gently.

I crumple the cat's tail into a ball in my fist. "Hurry."

But we're already speeding.

My fingertip finds a knot in the center of a flower on my dress. It goes round and round. I can see the clock in the car radio—00:53. It's past midnight. I stare at the glowing numbers, sobbing.

③

There's an exit ahead almost immediately. We'll go to a hospital. And I'll find a phone and call Mamma.

The car doesn't get into the exit lane. It doesn't slow down. What's the matter with the old man? Daddy doesn't drive this way.

We pass the exit ramp. "Why aren't we getting off?" My words are lost in the noise of the motor and the wind. These men don't have air-conditioning; their windows are open. I scoot forward onto the edge of the seat and speak loudly. "We have to go to a hospital. Or the police. Why aren't we going to the police?"

The young man takes a bag off the floor by his feet. He reaches in and hands me something. It's an apricot. He says a few words.

"I don't know what you're saying. Take me to the police."

He talks softly.

My head hurts. My eyes burn and I'm tired and all I want is to talk to Mamma on the phone, to get her to come here and make everything right again.

The man says something more, and I can tell he's worried. I can tell he's trying to be nice, trying to keep me calm. He turns and looks ahead again.

All right, so he told me something. Maybe that the police station is at the next exit. Maybe something like that.

I stay on the edge of the backseat and clutch the apricot. There are no signs, no more exits. We're driving fast. I peek over the old man's shoulder—100. My heart jumps. But that's kilometers, not miles. Daddy told me about kilometers. There's almost two to a mile. So we're not going so fast, after all. Maybe it just seemed extra fast because of the open windows. There aren't many cars on the road now, mostly trucks. People in cars have gone home by now.

I move to my window, the right window, and blink my eyes against the wind. I want to see it way ahead of time.

There it is: another exit coming up. I tap the young man on the shoulder.

He turns to me.

"There's another exit," I say. I point to the sign. I jab my finger insistently in the air.

The man looks ahead, as though he's trying to follow my finger and figure out what I mean. He turns back to me and speaks with eyebrows lowered. He has a cleft in his chin. The old man looks briefly at us. He has a cleft, too. The old man says something. They argue. And the younger man calls the old man *Papà*. I knew it: The old man is his father. I could tell.

They're still arguing and no one's paying attention to the road.

"Take the exit," I say loudly. "Take me to the police."

They stop arguing.

We don't get into the exit lane.

"The exit!" I practically shout. "Get over."

They keep looking ahead.

"What are you doing? Get over! Please, please get over." I grab the old man's shoulder and shake. He just drives. They're not taking me to the police. Oh, they're not taking me to the police. Where are they taking me?

I scream as we pass the exit. I scream and scream.

The son puts his finger to his mouth in the hush sign.

I scream in his face.

He puts his hand over my mouth.

I fall back against the seat on the left side, out of his reach, and scream.

He rolls his window up. The old man rolls his up,

too. They argue again. The son turns on the radio loud.
I can hear it because I'm not screaming anymore. I'm just
sitting. Sitting in a car with two strangers. Going who
knows where.

Now I remember the first car that stopped after
Daddy pulled off the road. It was white. With two men
in the front, arguing. It was them. I'm sure of it.

I clench my teeth and hug myself and squeeze as
hard as I can. These men saw me—they saw a girl alone
on the highway. And they came back. They came for
me. They argued about it—then they came for me.

Who are they?

I swallow and my ears pop. My throat hurts. My
eyes hurt. I feel like I haven't slept in a million years.
Then I remember: Mamma would want me to wear the
seat belt. She would want me to stay alive. I feel around,
but I can find only one side. The other must be caught
under the seat.

If I lie down, maybe I'll be safer. Newspapers and
junk clutter the seat, but I'm afraid to push them out of
the way. I don't want the son to turn back and look at
me. I never want him to touch me again.

I put the apricot on the floor and lie on my right side
on top of all the mess. If I stay very still, maybe I won't
wrinkle my dress too bad. Mamma will want me to look

neat on the airplane home. I clutch the stupid toy cat against my chest and close my eyes. Tears leak across the bridge of my nose, across my right temple, into my hair.

I open my eyes to light. I'm in the backseat of a parked car. Flies circle around the junk that surrounds me. And now it all comes back.

Daddy.

Daddy and those two men.

I sit up.

The son is leaning in through a window. He's staring at me. I get the creepy feeling he's been staring at me for a while. But now he blinks, as though in surprise. He smiles and talks.

"Eh?" The old man was asleep in the driver's seat. He shakes his head and looks from me to his son.

The son opens the car door and pulls the seat forward.

I'm fully awake now. I climb out, careful not to brush his hand. We're pulled over on the side of a dirt road. Fields of something green surround us. Spinach, maybe. Something like that. Immediately I need to go to the bathroom. I look at the son and grimace, with my hands squeezed between my knees.

"*Pipì?*" he says.

I nod. This is one word I understand totally.

He flicks the back of his hand toward the field.

I run between two rows of green as far as I can make it before I absolutely have to squat. The dew from the plants on either side wets my arms.

Dew. It's morning.

How long did we drive?

Where am I?

It was close to 1:00 A.M. when the men picked me up. And they were going a little over fifty miles an hour. I wish I knew what time it was now—but it's full morning, I know that. So we could have traveled six or seven hours at least. If we kept going straight, we're now deep in the south of Italy.

Daddy loves the south of Italy. He said the people are friendlier here.

Friendly.

These men picked me up and took me far away from everyone. There's nothing friendly about them.

I swallow and swallow. My throat hurts bad from all the screaming I did last night. But I keep swallowing. I feel like I'll shatter if I don't—just fall apart in tiny pieces.

The son calls out. He stands at the end of the field and looks down between the rows at me. He takes a step into the dirt.

I stand quickly. I can't see anything in any direction. Nothing but fields. No houses. Nowhere to hide. It doesn't make sense to even try.

But I do. I run up the row as fast as I can.

I hear footsteps louder than my own. I know the son's about to catch me the instant before he grabs my elbow and spins me around. I scream and hit him with both fists in the center of his chest.

He pulls me to him and holds me tight.

I stamp on his feet and thrash.

He turns me around so my back is to him and half carries, half drags me toward the car.

I scream and kick.

Then I stop. I let myself hang heavy, as though I'm a giant sack of sugar or something, as though I'm not me. For a moment I wonder if I'm dreaming. If only I'm dreaming.

The son puts me down beside the car. He stands at the ready, but he doesn't yell at me. He doesn't say a word.

When I don't move, he reaches into a bag in the car, takes out a roll with powdered sugar on top, and hands it to me. Then he hands me another apricot. He motions for me to get back in the car.

I look up and down the empty road. How can there be no cars all this time? Not one. I climb in.

The son gets in the front passenger seat and closes the door.

The old man appears from the field across the road. He gets in the driver's seat and turns the car around.

The men munch their rolls. The smell overwhelms me. I'm suddenly savagely hungry. I eat my roll. It's fresh and sweet. They must have stopped and bought these rolls while I was sleeping. They're so soft.

I watch the men from behind. I don't understand what's going on. They didn't take me to a hospital or the police. So they're dangerous. I'm old enough to know that. But neither of them is mean to me. Neither has been mean to me the whole time. Even when I was screaming. Even when I hit the young man and stamped on his feet.

I move into the right corner of the car and look out at the road ahead. "Where are we going?"

The young man turns on the radio loud. He offers an open white bag to me. I don't touch it, but I look in. More sweet rolls. Some of them have chocolate filling that spills out one end. I take one of those. The chocolate is slightly melted. I don't want to like it, but I do— it's delicious.

A small truck passes, going in the other direction. I didn't see it or hear it. I was busy eating.

And the radio is loud.

Did the young man turn on the radio so I wouldn't notice the truck? Like he turned up the radio when I screamed last night?

I let down my guard for a moment. I can't do that. I won't eat any more rolls. The radio won't trick me again.

The dirt road comes out onto a narrow paved country road. We drive faster now.

"Where are you taking me?" I lean toward the back of the young man's head. I whisper, "What do you want?"

The son looks back at me and stretches out his arm to pick up the toy cat that's fallen onto the floor. He tosses it onto my lap with a smile. I hate that he smiles at me. Does he think I'm an idiot, that I'd be fooled by a smile?

The car pulls over near a bridge. The old man turns down the radio. He says something roughly to his son. They talk quickly.

I'm thirsty now. And I feel dirty. "Hurry," I say. Wherever we're going, there's got to be a phone there. I'll find it. I'll get help. "Please hurry."

The old man glances at me. Then he gets out of the car, leaving the engine running, and walks out onto the bridge. He throws something into the water.

I move to the left side and sit forward on the seat. From this angle I can see both the old man's hand and the surface of the water. I can see what he throws; it's dark blue. It slaps onto the surface of the water and rides there for a little, then gets pulled under with the current.

It was a passport. I'm sure of it.

Daddy's way back somewhere hours and hours ago in the car, and I'm lost, and the old man just threw away a passport.

Maybe my passport.

I feel like I'm gone—like I sank with that passport. I feel sick.

I know I can't outrun the son. He already proved that. But we're on a paved road. A car should come along any moment.

I push the empty driver's seat forward and jump out and run along the street. I'll stop a passing car. There has to be a passing car. One has to come now. One has to.

The son catches me around the waist and lifts me high, holding me firm with my back to him. He speaks into my ear.

I twist my head and bite his neck, as hard as I can.

He lets out a yelp and pulls on my hair till I have to stop biting. I kick, but he just tilts me so that my legs thrash in the air. He carries me back to the car and gets in the backseat with me. He's on the right side and I'm in the middle now, and one of his hands is still holding onto my hair, controlling my head, while the other pins me to him.

The old man takes off. The car bounces in potholes. For a moment the world goes hazy and I feel pressure inside my head, inside my eardrums again, but this time I feel like my whole head will pop. Then the noise of the world comes back and I can think again.

I stop fighting. It's a waste of energy. I'll wait till I see an opportunity, then I'll do whatever makes sense. But I'll look around carefully first the next time. I'll plan things right. I've already had two strikes. I won't risk a third.

I'm panting.

The son still holds me tight, even though I'm not moving anymore. He talks now. He talks on and on. After a while, he lets go of my hair and pets my head. He says, "Antonia." His voice breaks. "Antonia." He speaks very softly now, on and on and on. He sounds so sad, I can't help thinking about Daddy. I swallow.

The car turns onto a ramp for a highway. There's a ticket booth up ahead. I'll scream when the car stops at the ticket booth. I'll scream as loud as I can. Even if the old man turns up the radio, someone outside this car will hear me, especially with the windows open like they are now.

The car slows, but it doesn't stop. It goes through the rightmost lane, and the old man doesn't even get a ticket. It must be one of those electronic lanes that Daddy talked about. We don't have them in Minnesota. Our roads are free.

I love Minnesota. I hate Italy.

I sink back against the son in defeat. His arm relaxes a little. Both of us had tensed up. He must have guessed my plan.

I read a lot. And I've seen a lot of movies. If I'm going to get away from these men, I have to come up with a plan they can't guess.

The highway is busy. Most of the cars and trucks go faster than us. A car goes by with a little kid jumping free on the backseat. Maybe a policeman will stop them to give them a ticket. I can recognize Italian police cars—they all have *polizia* written on them. But I watch and watch, and I still don't see any police cars.

I look up at the son and slide away from him, leaving a patch of seat between us. He lets me, but he takes hold of my hand. "Why?" I ask him. "Why did you take me? Where are we going?"

He reaches into his pocket and pulls out a pack of gum. He offers it almost shyly.

I won't allow him to think he's being nice. Nothing

about this is nice. I turn my head and look out the window.

Has anyone found Daddy yet?

If they have, then they're looking for me. They're looking for me right now, I bet.

Only, if that was my passport that the old man threw in the river, then they don't know that I was traveling with Daddy. There was nothing of mine in the car—nothing but the toy cat. And these men brought the toy cat with us.

No one's looking for me.

Unless they called Mamma. She'd tell them I was with him. Poor Mamma. She must be so scared.

I have to get away from these men for her sake. For Mamma. I have to think of a way—for Mamma.

And for me.

(4)

The car gets into the exit lane. I didn't expect that.

We've been driving for hours and my ears have been popping nonstop. We're high in the mountains. The noise of the straining motor of this little car has grown so loud, I feel like it's inside my head.

This exit mustn't get a lot of traffic, because there are only two lanes at the ticket booth. One booth has a man and the other must be just for cars to drive through—electronic, like the entry ramp lane we went through before. There aren't any cars ahead of us. If I shout, the man at the booth in the other lane will hear me. He has to.

We're close. My skin itches with anticipation. I want to scream now. But I have to stop myself till we're closer, till the last possible minute, so the man in the booth will hear me. Soon.

The son shoves the toy cat in my face as the car lurches forward. We zoom through the electronic lane. I'm spluttering and gasping as he takes the cat away from my face.

They aren't stupid.

Neither am I.

Mrs. Ronberg, the art teacher in my school, says my work is organized and systematic. She never calls me creative. It sort of bothers me, but not really. I'd rather be organized and systematic. I'm a science type. Everyone says that. I guess that's part of being practical—like Mamma calls me. But I have to be creative now if I'm going to get away.

I'm going to get away.

We drive a long time again, on a curving two-lane road through forests and orchards and farmlands. The road runs uphill and down, but mainly down. I can feel it in my ears. In America, Daddy would drive slowly on a road like this. But the old man doesn't slow down at all. He speeds past cars and small trucks full of farm produce. He even speeds through places where the street is lined on both sides by drab gray houses that share their side walls. Like in Rome. I thought Rome was that way because it's so crowded. But even these tiny villages have no space between the houses. They look poor. The masonry is rough. Sometimes open doorways are covered with ugly hanging strips of plastic in bright colors. The old man honks his horn before he rounds each curve, but he doesn't slow down.

And now there's a long stretch of wild land.

The old man pulls the car off the road, right into the trees, and stops. He turns the engine off.

The son is shaking his head and talking so fast, spit flies out of his mouth. I'm sure he's telling his father to get back on the road. He keeps moving his hands like that.

But the old man gets out of the car. He gestures for us to get out, too.

The son pulls me next to him and holds me tight again. He shouts something at the old man, but he doesn't budge.

I don't know what's going on. It's as though the young man wants to keep us on the road because he's got a plan. As though this whole thing is his idea. But the old man has his own idea. What? There's nothing here but woods. There can't be any good reason why the old man stopped.

I realize now that the old man has never said any-thing to me. He's never smiled at me. I don't like his son—I hate his son—but at least he treats me like I'm a person.

I'm not getting out of this car no matter what.

The old man throws his hand up at us in disgust. He walks around the car and opens the trunk. He's getting something out. I sit up tall and twist my whole body and crane my neck to look out the rear window. I want to see what it is. I have to see what it is. Even if it's horrible.

The old man shuts the trunk. He carries a checkered piece of cloth under one arm and a paper bag in his hand. He walks around to the small open area in front of the car, sets the bag down, and spreads the cloth on the ground, on top of all the undergrowth. Then he sits on the ground cross-legged and opens the bag.

The easy way he sits makes me understand he isn't as old as I thought he was. Not as old as Grandpa, for sure. His hair is as white as Grandpa's, but I bet he's a lot stronger. A little spasm of fear shoots through my chest.

The old man looks over his shoulder and calls something to us.

"No," says the son.

The old man takes out a package in white paper. He unwraps it. It's a sandwich—a long roll with lettuce sticking out the edges. He leans forward over the cloth and takes a bite. He looks off into the woods as he chews.

I can't believe it. He's stopped us here so that he can eat in peace. I could almost laugh with relief. But nothing's funny, really. The old man acts unpredictable. And unpredictable is scary.

I listen for cars on the road behind us.

The son shifts restlessly in his seat. Then he says something to the old man.

The old man makes that gesture of disgust with his hand again. He does it without even looking at us.

The son says it again, louder.

The old man puts his half-eaten sandwich on the tablecloth and stands. He carries the bag back to the car and hands it in to his son through the open front window. Then he goes back to the tablecloth, sits down, and picks up his sandwich.

The son lets go of me and opens the bag. He holds out a sandwich to me. When I don't take it, he puts it on my lap. Then he unwraps his sandwich and eats. He takes huge bites.

The strong smell of salami puts an end to whatever hunger I had. Hot salami. Those sandwiches must be half cooked—they've been sitting in the trunk since before I woke up this morning. Maybe since yesterday. Maybe the sun has made them go rotten, and these men will get sick and gag, and I'll be able to get out and run to the road and escape.

I look between the front seats at the clock on the radio: 14:13. It's after 2:00—long past lunchtime.

The son eats noisily. I refuse to look at him.

The old man has finished eating. He stands up, leans against a tree, and cleans his teeth with a toothpick.

Italians seem to love toothpicks. In restaurants I've seen lots of men pick their teeth after a meal. Before I thought it was just funny. Now it's gross.

The son crumples the empty paper from his sandwich and points at the sandwich on my lap. He says something even as he's chewing his last bite. I know he's asking if he can eat my sandwich. I wonder what difference it would make if I said no. But I put the sandwich in his hand quickly so that he won't take it off my lap himself.

The old man shakes out the tablecloth, folds it neatly, and puts it back in the trunk. Then he gets in the car, and we're on the road again, going faster even than before. That's how it feels, at least.

I move back to the far corner of the seat, behind the old man, and away from his son. How much longer can we keep going? Daddy said Italy was small. It doesn't seem small to me. It seems like it goes on forever.

So many wild areas with just trees and trees.

Finally I see a real town ahead. White buildings hug the hillside in continuous lines, like rows of seats in an auditorium, just curving outward instead of inward. The roofs are rust-colored tiles. A tall church stands high in the middle. Everything's so close together and there are so many houses that I'm sure someone would hear me if I shouted. Probably lots of people. The old man will have to slow down as he goes through this town. He'll have to.

I lean into my corner and close my eyes. If the son thinks I'm asleep, he won't push the toy cat in my face again. When I'm sure we're at the town, I'll spring forward and shout bloody murder.

But the car turns abruptly. I open my eyes. We're taking a side road away from the direction of the town. Within fifteen minutes, we're on a dirt road. Like the road near the field, when I woke up this morning. There's nothing around—no houses, no other cars. Nothing.

We climb on a zigzag path up a hillside. Low bushes are strung up on crossing-stick supports. I look closer. The bushes hold clusters of fruits—grapes. These are grapevines, like in the vineyard of the hotel Daddy and I stayed at. We climb high, going faster than my stomach can take. I keep swallowing nausea, even though I haven't eaten for hours.

The car turns again, and I see a house ahead. A lone white house with towering pine trees around it. I get ready to shout. Whoever is in that house will help me.

But we slow down till we stop in front of the house.

Oh, no—this was where we were going. This very house. No one inside there will help me.

We sit for a minute, none of us talking, just looking at the house. It's strange. The front door is two narrow doors that come together in the middle. A double door. And it isn't centered. Instead, it's off toward one end. The small windows on this side of the house are completely covered with shutters made of horizontal slats of wood. No one could see out or in.

The old man turns the key off. The engine coughs a few times and stops. He says something to his son.

The son draws me to him, his arm hard as a wood post. He says a few quick words in my ear. Then he gets out and stretches. A big purple bruise shows where I bit his neck the second time I tried to escape.

I'm alone in the backseat, breathing the dust that billowed when the car came to a halt. The old man is alone in the front seat.

It's hot here, even hotter than down at the base of the hill. It doesn't matter that the windows are open; the car bakes us. The only trees are those by the house, and we're not close enough to them to get any shade. I'm breathing through my mouth like my dog, Jersey.

The son goes to the house and in those front doors. He disappears inside the house.

I could run faster than the old man, I'm almost sure.

He may be strong, but I don't think he's fast. Still, I'd have to push the front seat forward and get out of the car first—and he could grab me at any point. Plus there's no other houses around. And no cars on the road. I've already learned how useless it is to run when there's nowhere to run to.

I look back at the house. Patches of white have fallen off here and there, and bricks show through underneath. It seems a thousand years old. And a thousand miles from anything.

This would be a perfect place to hide me.

For the first time I think of the terrible word: *kidnapped*. I've been kidnapped.

My cheeks twitch and I swallow again, swallow and swallow. Since last night I've been living in my worst nightmare. I want to roll time back, not let Daddy get sick, not let these men take me. I want to put us back in America, back in Minnesota, back with Mamma.

Instead, I'm here.

But why would anyone kidnap me? We're not rich. Maybe they don't know that. Or maybe it isn't money they want. People who kidnap can be horrible. Even if they give you sweet rolls and offer sandwiches.

I am sitting here waiting for what might be death.

When someone finally opens the door and pulls forward the front seat, I'll make a break for it. And if the son grabs me, I'll bite harder than ever. I'll kick and scream and stick my fingers in his eyes. I tense all my muscles, ready.

A woman bursts out of the house. She's Mamma's age, with reddish brown hair pulled back in a long ponytail and an angry look on her face. She rushes toward the car, then stops. She puts a hand over her eyes to shade against the sun and furrows her brows as she slowly comes forward, hunched over now, staring at me. She talks to the old man, but her eyes stay on me. She's shooting questions at him.

The old man speaks at last. His voice is annoyed and sort of whiny, like he's blaming someone. I bet I was right—I bet taking me was the young man's idea.

"Help me," I say to the woman. "Please, help me."

She talks to the man again, and I can make out the word *americana*. She's asking him about the fact that I'm American.

"Something happened to Daddy," I say. "And these men took me away."

The woman opens the door and pulls the seat forward. She reaches for my hand.

I don't know what to do. But she seems mad at the old man, and that has to be good. And I can't stand the heat in this car. I'll pass out if I stay here much longer. She must know that. She must want to help me, to keep

me safe. I take her hand and get out. The sun blinds me.
I bow my head immediately.

The woman leads me into the house. The cool dark
of the inside is a shock. Like entering a different world.
A calm world. It smells dry and woody. The furniture in
the living room is big and made of the darkest wood.
We go into a kitchen with a long table, and the woman
gestures me to sit down, so I do.

She pours me a drink.

I sniff. Then drink greedily. Cold lemonade. There's
a telephone on a side shelf. It's black and old and has a
funny shape. I quickly look away, so the woman won't
know I've been looking at it.

But she saw already. She picks up the phone and hesitates a moment. Then she places it on the table beside
me so hard that the phone gives a little ring. So she's
good. She's not a kidnapper. Maybe none of them are.
Maybe I just don't understand anything.

I lean over and curl my left arm around the phone,
cradling it. I lift the receiver. But I don't know how to
start. All right, I'll ask the operator. I've used a dial
phone before; I know how to do it. I put my finger into
the little hole over the zero and circle it around as far as
it can go. There. I did it. It's ringing.

A man's voice comes on, speaking Italian.

"Help me, please. I'm American. I have to call the United States."

The voice says, "One moment," in heavily accented English.

The son comes into the room and grabs the phone. He hangs up and puts it back on the shelf. He says something firmly to the woman. They argue. The only word I can pick out is *polizia*. She's shouting at him now. So he is bad. He really is. She's worried about the *polizia*—maybe she's even threatening to call them. I was so stupid to blow my chance—if I get another chance to use the phone, I'll dial zero and ask for the *polizia*.

The son puts his hand on the woman's shoulder. Nicely. As though he wants to comfort her. She backs away. He drops his arm. She stands there, shaking her head. He seems confused. He pleads with her.

I look around the room. A row of knives hangs from a magnetic strip near the sink. Weapons. I let my eyes pass on to the open window. I could never cut anyone.

Even if they were going to kill me?

My eyes go back to the knives.

The son unplugs the phone from the wall. The plug has big prongs on the end of it—so strange, like everything else here. He jams his hand into a pocket and comes out with a little crumpled box. It's the box from the candies Daddy gave me. He throws it on the table and says something more. His voice strangles on the words, as though he can hardly get them out, as though he's about to cry. Then he walks away, carrying the phone with him.

She watches him leave, standing so still, it seems she's asleep.

My eyes go back to the empty box of candies. The men really did remove every trace of me from Daddy's rental car. I go limp. I can't fight this. Not alone. I whisper to the woman, "Help me."

The woman looks at me. Her lips purse. She points to herself. "Claudia," she says. "Claudia." She points at me and raises an eyebrow.

"Jackie," I say.

"Jackie," she repeats, but it sounds funny. Sort of like Jeckie. She looks me up and down. She squats and examines my legs. I look down at streaks of blood and dirt caked together—the scrapes from when I fell in the highway last night. I didn't even remember them till now. And the skirt of my dress is ripped. The woman shakes her head ruefully. She says something in a gentle voice and walks toward another doorway—this kitchen has three.

I don't understand. But I don't want her leaving me

alone with the men, wherever they are now. I get up quickly and run to her.

We go down a corridor and into a bathroom. It's big and tiled in ceramics of mermaids, so beautiful—more beautiful even than the bathroom in our hotel. Daddy said Italy makes the best ceramic tiles. I'm surprised, though. Nothing about this house seems rich. And the car the men drove is all banged up. A little car with only two doors.

The woman turns on the tub water. She looks past her shoulder at me while she's bent over the faucet. She straightens up with sudden decision and opens a tall wooden cupboard standing on carved feet. She feels around in the back and says, "Ah," as she takes out a plastic bottle. She pours a glug of pink into the water. Bubbles form immediately. The air smells of strawberry. She puts back the bottle and says something to me. Then she turns off the water and leaves.

A bubble bath.

My clothes are dirty and rumpled, like me. My new dress is ruined. But I don't want to take it off. I don't want to be naked in this house.

The bubbles make little kissing noises as they pop. I bend over and put my hand in beneath the bubbles. It's just the right amount of hot.

Mamma makes me bubble baths when I'm blue. Like when I came in second in the spelling bee, but I should have come in first. I messed up on a silly word—*fallible*. It sounds a lot like *fail*, and it means that you make a mistake, so you fail. But it isn't spelled like *fail*.

The perfect word to mess up on. Daddy said it was ironic.

The woman comes back carrying a small stack of folded clothes with a little basket of purple grapes on top. "*Ecco*, Jackie," she says. She sets the clothes on the shelf beside the sink and holds out the grapes to me. "*Prego*." Her face begs me.

I eat one. It's cold and juicy. And it's been so long since I ate those sweet rolls with the men. "Thank you."

She keeps looking at me.

"Claudia," I add.

She closes her eyes for a moment and her mouth trembles. I think she's going to cry. First the man was on the edge of tears, now the woman—when I'm the one who's so sad, I'm the one who's in so much trouble. But when the woman opens her eyes, she smiles. Then she leaves, shutting the door firmly behind her.

I'm alone. Truly alone.

I set the basket of grapes on the floor, strip, step into the tub, and reach for the basket again. I hold it up close to my face. I remember the goblet in the restaurant last night—the beautiful clusters of glass grapes. I remember how much Daddy enjoyed his dessert. My daddy. My sweet, wonderful daddy, who laughs all the time and has such big, soft hands.

Daddy would like these grapes now. He'd like a good, hot bath.

The basket blurs as my tears well.

I put an icy grape in my mouth. Then another. I eat grapes, letting the hot water sap all my energy. Exhaustion melts me.

Daddy is gone.

I'm a prisoner.

(5)

The bubbles have all gone, and the surface of the water feels slippery. The water is cold now. Goose bumps form on my arms and chest, even though the air is hot. I get out, holding the empty basket, and drip on the tiled floor. There's a towel hanging on the back of the door, but it's used. I don't want to dry off with someone else's towel. But I don't want to stand here shivering, either. I back up against the towel, then turn slowly, letting it lightly rub me. The towel smells perfumed.

The clothes turn out to be a pair of blue underpants with fluffy white sheep on them, a pair of pink shorts, and a pale yellow shirt with pink shells that match the shorts. They fit pretty good, just a little bit big. Somebody here is close to my size.

Oh. That means somebody here might be my friend. Somebody might help me.

There's no mirror in this bathroom. How strange. I run my hands under the sink faucet, then work my fingers through my hair. I've got short, curly hair, so it doesn't take much to make it look all right.

Way above and behind the toilet is a window. It's tall because the ceiling is tall. It opens inward from the right side with a crank handle. Right now it's open only a crack. I close the toilet lid and stand on it so I can crank the window open wide. There's no screen, and I get the funny sensation that I'm about to fall, even though I've got firm footing where I'm standing.

The hill continues upward in one direction, but off to the right, beyond some fields, the land suddenly drops off. And way out there I see blue sky meeting green water. We're near the sea. I'm not sure how near— it could be miles—but that's definitely the sea. I live in Minnesota back home, where there are lots and lots of lakes. So I know, that's not lake water out there. Not that green.

I close the window to a crack again and go out into the corridor. After the sunlight of the bathroom, the corridor seems darker than ever. I wait to let my eyes adjust, and I listen.

Birds are singing really loud. It sounds like they're practically inside the house. I can't hear anything else. No voices.

Maybe they've left me. All of them. Alone in this house, far from anything except the sea.

It only takes a second before I realize the opportunity. I could get back in the bathroom and hoist myself up onto the ledge and jump out the window. It wasn't that far down, I don't think.

But maybe far enough to break a bone.

No, I'll try to go out through a door.

I step softly. The wide boards of the floor don't squeak at all. I'm going toward the kitchen, even though I'm pretty sure that if the woman is home, she'll be in the kitchen. I'm going in that direction because I don't know what lies in the other part of the house. And, at least, beyond the kitchen there's only one room to cross to get out the front door. Plus the kitchen had an open window, too. Maybe the drop is shorter there.

I peek into the kitchen, holding my breath. It's empty.

"Jackie."

I jump around to face her.

The woman, Claudia, comes from behind me in the corridor. She doesn't seem mad. Instead, her face seems to hang like an old person's—like she turned ten years older in the last half hour. She's looking at my shirt—at the shell designs on its scalloped edge. She pulls down on the hem, as though to neaten me up. She says something, more to herself than to me, of course. Now her fingers go to a little watch in a heart-shaped frame hanging from a chain around her neck. She didn't have it on before, or I would have noticed it, it's so pretty. Then she goes to the table. A pair of sneakers are sitting there. She picks them up and holds them out to me.

"Where is she?" I ask. "Where is the girl these clothes belong to?"

Claudia gives a tiny smile, as though she's apologizing for not understanding me. She puts the sneakers in my hands.

I don't like to wear sneakers without socks, even when it's hot. But my patent-leather shoes aren't anywhere in sight. "Socks?" I say. "Do you have any socks?" I point at my feet.

"*Che c'è?*" The old man comes into the kitchen. He takes the sneakers from me and shakes them at Claudia as he talks to her.

Claudia says something back to him, but it's different from how she talked to the son. She seems weaker somehow with the old man. And she's not angry at him; she's not fighting.

He gestures us back into the hall.

Claudia gives a little noise—a high-pitched cry. She takes my hand and leads me down the hall again, past the bathroom, to a door on the left. She opens it.

It's a bedroom, with a double bed. There's a big cabinet with tall doors standing on short carved legs, and a chair with a standing lamp beside it, and a table with a mirror. The walls are bare—no paintings, no photographs. But on the table is a brush with reddish brown strands of hair in it. This is Claudia's room.

She ushers us in and closes the door. Then she goes around to one side of the bed and lies down on top of the covers. She pats the bed beside her.

A nap?

Our hotel owner said midday naps are good for the digestion. He told us that's why so many businesses close after lunch and don't open again until four o'clock. But Daddy and I didn't take naps. We were usually too far from our hotel to be able to go back in the middle of the day. So we ducked into air-conditioned libraries or museums with high ceilings and big fans. And once we found a shady park with checkerboards painted onto concrete tables. There was only one complete set of checkers, so we had to wait for a couple of old men to finish. But then we got to play. It was so much fun.

The inside of my nose tingles. I squeeze my eyes shut to stop the tears. I don't want to think about playing checkers with Daddy. It hurts too much—and it makes me feel lost again, lost and weak. I have to be strong. I have to concentrate on getting away from here.

"Jackie," says Claudia. *"Vieni."*

I recognize that word from earlier. She said it when she led me to the tub. I'm guessing it means "come." I should pay closer attention when they talk. I should try to learn some Italian so I can figure out what's going on.

"Per favore, vieni." Her voice is warm and kind. I know *per favore*—it means "please."

I open my eyes and look at her. She gives a small smile and pats the bed again.

If I lie down beside her and pretend to sleep, maybe she'll fall asleep—and I can sneak out. Or maybe she'll think I'm sleeping and she'll leave—and I can sneak out.

It doesn't seem likely. But what else is there to try?

I lie down on the other side of the bed, careful to keep my arms close by my sides. A slight perfume comes from the pillow.

Claudia talks. But she isn't telling me what to do and she isn't asking questions. She just talks. On and on. So many words. And they come so fast. How on earth can I learn Italian fast enough? I can't make out a single word. And I finally realize that she's not really talking like a normal conversation. Her tone is different. She's telling a story. A bedtime story, maybe. As though I'm a little kid.

I didn't sleep much last night. And the tension of today has worn me down. Plus the bath left me feeling heavy. It's good to lie here.

I close my eyes and listen to the rhythm of the words.

Claudia's shaking me awake.

I rub my eyes and look at her. She puts her finger to her lips in the hush sign and whispers, *"Vieni, subito."* The way she says it electrifies me.

I follow her quickly out the door.

She closes it silently behind us. Then we go along the hall, to the kitchen.

The sneakers are sitting on the floor under the window. Claudia hands them to me.

I tie them on. They're tight. The girl these belong to must be younger than me. Or maybe she outgrew these sneakers last year.

Claudia hurries through the doorway that leads to the living room. I'm right behind her.

The dark of the living room makes me hesitate. But it's cool in here. That must be why they keep the shutters closed on this side of the house—to keep out the broiling sun. The other sides have the trees to do that. As soon as I adjust my eyes, I search for the phone. The son took it in here when he unplugged it. But I can't see it anywhere.

Claudia goes out the front door. I race across the room to the door. The white car is gone. I squint against the sun and look all around. There's no sign of either man. Where are they?

"Vieni," Claudia whispers. *"Sbrigati."* She walks out the path toward the dirt road.

I run and catch up, breathing hard with hope. Is she helping me to escape?

The path comes out ahead at a bend in the dirt road. Even from here I can see down the stretch of road below and up the stretch of road above. Not a single car is coming either way. And I bet there are no cars beyond the bends. My disappointment hurts. But what could I have been thinking? If a lot of cars came this way, the road would be paved.

I don't need a lot of cars, anyway. I need one. One car of people who will help me. That's why Claudia brought me out here. It must be.

I take a deep breath, and despite everything, I feel almost happy. It's so good to be outside and away from the men. We're going to get free.

We're almost at the end of the path, almost out on the dirt road that I drove on before, when Claudia turns right. What's she doing? I want to keep going straight, out to that road.

"Vieni," she calls.

Okay, I'll at least see what's going on. I'm at her heels immediately, swatting at the small flies that have come from nowhere. There are steps cut into the hillside. The road zigzags way to the left, then way to the right, but the steps go down in a steep, straight line as far as I can see. Oh, yes, Claudia was right: This will be much faster than walking the zigzag of the road. And if we hear a car coming on the road, we can jump high and flag it down and then run across the rows of grapevines to the nearest section of road. This is a good plan.

I race ahead of Claudia.

I think of the paved road at the bottom of this hill, the road that leads to the town I saw when we drove here. There are *polizia* and telephones in that town. Even if no car comes down the dirt road of the hill, even if no car comes along once we reach the paved road at the bottom, we can walk to the town. We're strong. I'm practically flying down the hillside.

A snake lies on the step right in front of me.

I stop so fast, my sneakers slide in the dirt and I almost skid off the edge of the step down onto the snake below.

It's gray with two black stripes running its full length. Its tail seems to be twisted over itself, almost as though it's in a knot.

I don't move.

Italy has poisonous snakes. And spiders. And scorpions. The airline magazine on the flight over had a big article about them. It was titled "The Three Scary S's of Italy." Daddy said it was stupid to put a story about something scary in a travel magazine. He didn't read it. But I did. I read the whole article. Just reading it made my skin crawl. I hate snakes. I hate them, I hate them.

This snake's head is small. Poisonous snakes usually have big heads. But it's long. A snake's striking distance depends on how long it is.

Okay, think. The important thing is not to move quickly. Not to make it strike, if it's the kind of snake that strikes.

I step backward up to the next step behind me as slowly as I can.

The snake flicks its tongue.

I barely breathe.

All of a sudden it zips off the step and into the rows of grapevines below. It didn't take it even a second to unravel that tail.

I turn to run back up the path when Claudia catches up to me.

I point. "A snake."

Claudia passes me and stoops beside the faintest

track that the snake left in the dirt. She wrinkles her nose and pinches it, as though something smells bad. Then she holds out her hand toward me. She wants to keep going down the steps.

But I don't want to go on the steps anymore. The snake went down the hill. It could come out on a lower step.

I look around. A bend in the dirt road comes close to the steps here. We can easily walk along a row of grapevines and be out on that road in a couple of minutes. I take Claudia's hand and pull her toward the road.

She talks a lot.

"I won't go where the snake went," I say. "Let's take the road. I don't care if it's longer." I pull her toward the road, harder.

She's not very big. Shorter than Mamma. Thinner, too. But her arms are muscled and her hands feel rough. She doesn't have to yield to me. But she does. Gratitude fills me. I squeeze her hand briefly.

We walk a short distance through the vines, with me looking around carefully for other snakes, and come out on the road. We pass the bend and walk quickly. Within fifteen minutes I hear a motor. It whines as it comes down the hillside from above us. I'm so excited.

I look at Claudia. Her face is frozen in worry. She

turns and runs into the vines and stoops. *"Vieni,"* she calls, gesturing quickly. *"Vieni,* Jackie."

I don't want to hide. Whoever is coming down the hill will help me.

But, oh, what if it's the men? Maybe that's why Claudia's hiding. Maybe that's why she wanted to take the steps in the first place. I run into the vines beside her.

A small truck with an open flatbed comes around the bend. It's blue and old and even more beat-up than the men's white car.

Claudia shakes her head and lets out a groan. I stand, but she grabs my hand and tugs me back down.

But this isn't the men—it's a noisy little truck. And now I realize that Claudia must have known it wasn't the men, because the truck's motor is so much louder than the men's car. Even I should have realized that.

I don't know why Claudia's acting like this. I don't know who to trust.

But I have to take any chance I get. Mamma would want me to. I jump up and wave my free hand and shout, "Help."

The truck screeches to a halt. A man with a little cap on his head looks out at me. He says something.

Claudia stands up behind me and answers him.

The man grins. "Claudia, *la bellissima,"* he says. He

gets out of the truck and comes around the front of it to the edge of the road.

Claudia holds my hand tight. She bites her bottom lip and says something to me.

The man looks at her, then at me. He knows Claudia—he said her name. But they're obviously not friends.

I could break free of Claudia and run to this man and tell him to take me to the *polizia*, but there's something in his look that stops me. His grin isn't a happy one. It's more like a leer. And the way he's standing is almost like he's getting ready for a fight, like he's going to pounce. I don't like anything about him.

I step halfway behind Claudia.

The man comes toward us through the vines. He's talking as he comes. His voice teases in an unpleasant singsong. And he keeps leering at Claudia. He's close now.

She talks harshly to him and suddenly hurries past him, pulling me along on the side away from him. His arm circles her waist. She snaps her head at him, fast as that snake, and jerks herself free.

We're out on the road now. We go down, the same direction we were going before. I stay at Claudia's side, holding fast to her hand. I'm thinking about this man's arm around her waist, about the way her eyes went wide for an instant. The thought makes me feel sick. He's nasty.

He says something from behind us. He repeats it.

Claudia's hand squeezes mine. She moves faster. I'm practically running to keep up. Is he following us? Claudia looks straight ahead. But I can't help it; I look back over my shoulder.

The man sets his feet wide apart and watches us. Then he laughs and gets in his truck again.

"He's coming," I say in a panic. "He's coming, he's coming."

Claudia puts one arm around my back and up under my arm and marches along the road at the same pace, practically lifting me along.

The truck comes up behind us and the man honks.

I look back at him. He's honking in my face. He grins that dirty, dirty grin. I can't take my eyes off him. But Claudia won't even look at him.

I understand. Claudia doesn't want to give in to him. She won't show she's afraid, because that would only make him act worse. That's how bullies are. I know. In every grade some kids are bullies. That's just how it is. The best thing to do is ignore them.

So I shouldn't keep looking at him. But I have to. He's horrible.

What's the matter with the men around here? Are they all strange?

If only another car would come along to frighten off the man. But no cars come. No one travels on this road.

Something inside me is crumbling.

I can't stand this. I want Daddy. I never should have left him in the car. This is what I get for abandoning him. I'm sorry, Daddy. I didn't know what else to do. I was scared. Like I am now. I want Mamma. I can't stand it anymore. You. Then those two men. Now this truck driver. One bad thing after another. I am going to scream. I am going to explode.

And now there's a different horn. I turn my head forward and see the white car pull up in front of us. The son is driving. He's alone. The engine coughs and stops. The son gets out and says something angry to Claudia.

Claudia just looks at him, but her mouth trembles, like it did when she prepared the tub for me. She really was trying to help me escape—I'm sure of it. Her arm stays strong around my back, but her chest deflates. She feels defeated, I can tell. I don't want her to feel defeated. I want her to fight—to fight for me.

The man in the truck swings out and around us and takes off fast.

The three of us get into the white car and head back up the hillside, back toward the white house.

6

No one says anything until we're back at the house and in the kitchen. Then the son talks. He says something and takes a loaf of bread out of a big bag— one of those long loaves that isn't in slices. He says something more and takes out a round yellowish ball. He says something more and takes out a square wrapped in brown paper with string holding it shut. Each time he speaks, it's like a bark. He's mad. And I hear something else in his voice. I think it's fear.

Claudia waits till he stops talking. Then she talks. She says my name. She says *americana*. She says *mamma*. I know she's telling him I'm American and he should give me back to my mother. I know it. Claudia has to win this argument. My stomach knots. In an instant they're shouting at each other.

The old man comes in from the hall, obviously having been woken by their yelling. He pulls a shirt on over his sleeveless undershirt as he walks in. He says, *"Zitti!"* very loud. Claudia and the son hush. Now he talks firmly to both of them.

The son hesitates, then leaves.

Claudia doesn't move. The old man points down the hall. Claudia looks at me, then she puts the yellowish ball in the refrigerator and leaves. The fight is over, just like that. It's strange how Claudia obeys the old man, almost like a child sent to her room.

I'm left alone with the old man. This can't be. Of the three of them, he's the one I have the least sense of. Why did he stop their fight? He doesn't want me here. He never even looks at me. Why doesn't he side with Claudia against his son? But I can't ask him. And I don't want to be near him.

I hurry after Claudia, but the old man says something to me. He gestures for us to go into the living room. And I know I'm supposed to do what he tells me. Everyone seems to do whatever he says.

He goes into the dark living room and turns on the television. He calls me over. His voice is softer now.

I stand in the kitchen doorway and watch him, uncertain of what to do. I'd make a break for the door, except I know the son is somewhere around. Lurking.

The old man clears his throat and calls me again, this time almost nicely.

I come in slowly and stand by the couch where he's sitting.

He points toward the television with a little motion of his chin. He asks me something.

There's a soccer game on television. I don't play soccer, but my friend Noëlle does, so I've seen some of her games. This is men's soccer. The ball moves really fast.

A player falls, and the referee blows his whistle. The old man lets out a hoot and slaps his knee. He says something to me, all excited.

I stand there and look slowly around the room. A fairly ugly painting of a seashore with fat little kids running along the sand hangs over the couch. There's a fireplace on the next wall, with a vase full of fresh wildflowers on the mantel. Standing on either side of the vase are groups of small photographs in fancy gilded frames. They look old, but I really can't tell that much from here.

The old man makes another exclamation about the soccer game. He seems completely absorbed. I remember how he insisted on getting out of the car at lunchtime to spread the tablecloth on the ground and eat his sandwich. There he had a prisoner in his car, and he still wanted his picnic, all the same. And now he has that same prisoner in his house, but he wants to watch his soccer game.

Mamma always says I like my routines too much. In fact, she said one reason it would be good for me to go on this trip with Daddy was so that I could break out of my routines.

But I'm nothing compared to the old man. He loves his routines.

I'm almost sure that he won't care what I do now, so long as I don't bother his soccer game. So I walk over to the fireplace and look at the photos. One is of a young man and woman with three children—a girl and two smaller boys. The next one is of a teenage girl. Her hair is short and frizzy and her face is fatter than it is now, but it's Claudia, I can see that. I look back at the photo of the family again. Yes, the girl in that photo is Claudia, too. She was younger than me there—maybe eight or nine, but it's her.

The next photo is of a teenage boy.

Beyond the vase there are three more photos. The first one is of another teenage boy—but I recognize this one—it's the son. Maybe ten years ago, but that's him. And, oh—I look back at the photo of the family—maybe that little boy on Claudia's lap in the family photo is the son, too.

I turn my head to look quickly at the old man on the couch. It's hard to see a resemblance between him and Claudia, but maybe. Maybe.

He must notice me out of the corner of his eye, because he pulls his attention away from the television and glances at me.

"Are you Claudia's daddy—her *papà*—too?" I ask.

He puts his index finger to his chest. *"Papà di Claudia, sì."* He nods, then looks back at the television and practically shouts at the referee.

So I'm here with Claudia and her father and brother. It makes me glad to know the young man is Claudia's brother. I would have hated it if she was married to him. But, then, he's too young for her, anyway.

But now I'm having even more trouble figuring out what's going on. None of it makes sense. They seem like an ordinary family—ordinary people. Not criminals at all. Why did the men bring me here? They don't seem to want anything from me. This all feels confused, like some giant mistake. Some giant misunderstanding. Oh, if only that's all it was.

I put my hand on the mantel and look at the last two photos. A baby in a young man's arms—I don't recognize either of them. And a little girl of maybe four or five years old with the old man and an old woman. I'm pretty sure the old woman is just an older version of the woman in the family photo on the far end—Claudia's mother.

I walk around the room, but there's nothing else interesting.

"Eh," grunts the old man. He pats the couch beside him, like Claudia patted the bed when she wanted me to nap with her. He grunts again. That's funny. Claudia talks to me normally and just pretends I understand. The old man, instead, won't talk to me at all. He seems like a caveman. Like in the days before people used language. When I don't move, he picks up the remote control and holds it out toward me. He shakes it. Finally, he says something coaxing.

I can't believe it: He's offering to let me choose the channel. Why? He acted like that soccer game was the most thrilling thing in the world. But he's willing to stop watching it if I want something else.

I don't get it.

The old man keeps holding the remote control out toward me with his right hand. The corner of his mouth rises into a small half smile. He says very softly, *"Per favore."*

I don't want the old man to be nice to me. He should go back to caveman grunts. He shouldn't say "please." He shouldn't say anything kind. I want to hate him. I feel like I'm going to cry again.

In a burst, I walk over and take the remote and change the channel. Some stupid news comes on. Talk I don't understand. I change channels again. I'll find something the old man hates. I change until I get to an old rerun of *Bewitched*. It's dubbed into Italian. The old man is bound to think it's really stupid. I sit down on the end of the couch as far from the old man as possible and hold the remote control, almost daring him to grab it from me and switch back to his beloved soccer game. I'll prove to him that he's not nice—he's a big phony.

The old man keeps that smile.

We sit there watching *Bewitched*.

The old man relaxes into the cushions of the couch like he's totally comfortable. As though this is normal. As though we're supposed to be side by side.

As though I live here.

He must be crazy.

None of this feels real.

Claudia calls us from the kitchen.

Her voice comes like an interruption from far away. I feel like I've just been woken up. The old man and I have been watching television for a long time. When *Bewitched* ended, an old *Simpsons* came on. Then a long and complicated bunch of commercials. I couldn't figure out what was being advertised at all. Then some show that

I've never seen before. It was made in Italy, I'm sure, because the voices matched the movement of the lips. And it must have been funny, because the old man laughed a few times.

But now the old man takes the remote from me and clicks off the television. He stands up.

And we're back to the world again. We're here, in Italy, where I don't belong.

The old man waits for me to get up. So I walk into the kitchen, with him behind me.

Claudia stands by the table with a knife in her hand. The son—her brother—leans against the door frame on the other side of the kitchen, watching her. He seems different—relaxed. And he's looking at Claudia with love. As though he adores his big sister. She cuts the string on the brown paper package that he took out of the bag when he came home in the car. She unwraps a square of thick-crust pizza.

The hotel Daddy and I stayed at served me that kind of pizza for breakfast.

Sadness stabs me. I miss Daddy. I miss my daddy so much. I let myself drop into a chair.

Claudia looks at me. Her hands go to her cheeks. Then she picks me up and sits, with me on her lap. I'm too old to sit on laps. But I don't want to get off Claudia's lap. I'm heaving, using all my energy to hold back tears. Claudia's chest rises and falls, as though she's crying, but her eyes are dry, too.

The brother takes a knife from the metallic holder by the sink and gets the yellow ball out of the refrigerator. He cuts a wedge. I can see now that it's cheese. He rips off a hunk of bread and puts the bread and cheese on a plate in front of Claudia and me. When neither of us reacts, he pushes it closer and smiles. Then he sweeps the bits of crust from ripping the bread into his hand and eats them.

A flowery cloth serves as a cover to a box under the window. He pulls the cloth away. The box is full of fat tomatoes. He picks out three and washes them in the sink. He washes them with soap. I've never seen anyone wash food with soap. Then he slices them very thin, equally into four bowls. He pours green-yellow oil on top and sprinkles pinches of salt from a small wooden bowl on the shelf. He puts a fork in each bowl and sits down to eat from one.

All his movements are strong and purposeful, and I find myself paying attention. I can't take my eyes from him, just like I couldn't take my eyes from the man in the blue truck as he followed Claudia and me, honking. Only now there's another reason I watch: I'm hungry. The only thing I've eaten since the sweet rolls this morning was that bunch of grapes in the tub. I sniffle back the last of my tears and stand up. I'm very, very hungry. I'm completely famished.

I take a bowl of tomatoes and sit on a chair and eat. They're ripe and wonderful.

The old man—the father—sits down across from me and says something to me.

I don't look at him. I won't let him think that just because we watched television together we're now friends. Friends. How could he think we'd ever be friends?

Claudia cuts the thinnest sliver of cheese and holds it out to me.

It smells sharp. At home Mamma buys sharp cheddar and I like that. But some of the Italian cheeses I tasted with Daddy weren't so good. I bite this cheese hesitantly. It's all right.

Claudia cuts me a few more thin slices and gets me a plate and a piece of bread.

The brother pushes the pizza toward me. There's only one slice—and it isn't cut into pieces. He says something. I get the feeling he bought this one slice of pizza just for me. But I won't touch it. I won't let him think he's being nice to me, just like I won't let the father think he's being nice to me. Not ever. They took me away when they shouldn't have.

They know they're wrong. Anyone knows that.

We eat in silence.

But birds are singing again. Or not really singing—sort of squabbling. I'm sure they're in this house somewhere.

The brother leans back in his chair, one hand still on the table. He sighs loudly.

Claudia puts her hand on his. She pats it. She loves him, too. For a moment their faces are calm and their expressions are the same. It's as though someone painted them and could do only one face. But Claudia's eyes are even sadder than her brother's. They look as sad as I feel.

The brother pulls his hand away and says something, not yelling or anything, but the tone tells me it's an order. Claudia glances at me. So the order is about me. I clench my teeth.

Now they're all talking. I listen hard, but I can't catch any words, not even my name. Maybe they're talking about something else. The brother points at the wall clock by the table. It says 9:22. How did it get to be so late?

We finish eating, and Claudia takes me by the hand. She doesn't even clean up the dishes—she just leads me to the bathroom and waits outside for me. Then she takes me to her bedroom. So that was it? Her brother told her to put me to bed? Only that? But who put him in charge? How come Claudia listens to her little brother?

I look around. One side of the bedcovers is folded down, and on the pillow there's a nightgown. Claudia walks over and holds it out to me. It's white and sleeveless, and I can tell it goes all the way to the ground. Tiny roses ring the neckline, but otherwise it's just white, like a cloud. It's perfect.

I touch the roses, one by one. "Where is she?" I ask.

Claudia looks at me as though she understands, as though she's searching for words.

"I want to meet her." And I want to befriend her, I think. And I want to get her to help me. This girl, whoever she is, will understand what a mess I'm in. She'll know I need to get back to Mamma. She'll know how to sneak out of here without being bitten by snakes, without being followed by the man in the blue truck.

Claudia lays the nightgown back on the pillow. She goes over to the chair and sits and talks. She talks on and on—oh, she's telling me a story again, like she did before the nap today. I stand there watching her, listening, even though I have no idea what she's saying, as the room grows slowly darker. Finally, she gets up and leaves, closing the door behind her.

Will she come back in and sleep with me?

I don't want to sleep with her.

But I don't want to sleep alone, either. There's a comfort in being with Claudia. Her voice makes me feel better.

I put on the nightgown and lay my folded clothes on the chair. I climb into bed.

I can't hear anything from the kitchen. I don't know what the rest of them are doing. I don't know what they're planning.

But I have a plan. I'll wait till the middle of the night, till they're all asleep. Then I'll tiptoe outside and walk all the way to the town. I'll take the dirt road. It'll be deserted. I can do it. The shutters over the window are closed, but I remember watching the moon with Daddy a couple of nights ago. It was almost full. Moonlight will guide me.

It'll be okay.

The perfume of the pillow surrounds me. I think it's rosewater. The nightgown feels silky soft.

(7)

I wake to the sound of a toilet flushing.

How long was I asleep?

My eyes adjust to the dark. Oh, no, it isn't that dark—it isn't as dark as it was when I went to bed. But it can't be morning yet, please, I can't have slept all night—no, please, no.

Claudia's not beside me. Her side of the bed is still made.

I stand up. The wood floor feels smooth under my bare feet. I pad over to the window. But it's not obvious how to open the shutter. I go to the chair, where my clothes wait, and I dress. Then I open the door just a crack. Light comes from the kitchen. There's no one in the hall.

I go out into the hall slowly, ready to bolt back to

Claudia's bedroom if I hear anyone. I stand there a minute, then I walk toward the kitchen.

The bathroom door is ajar. It's empty. I slip in and close the door. When I finish up, I don't know whether to flush or not. Flushing is loud. But it seems awful not to. I flush.

When I go out into the hall again, it's still empty. I walk quietly to the kitchen.

Claudia sits with her elbows on the table and her forehead resting in her hands. Between her elbows is a cup of coffee. The smell is rich and strong. There are dirty plates and cups on the table. Everyone rose early.

But Claudia must have just woken up, because she's wearing a nightgown and her hair is loose. I wonder where she slept.

Morning sun floods the room. I look at the wall clock. It's almost nine—not early at all. I can't believe I slept that long, especially after I took a nap yesterday.

From the living room come the sounds of the television. I can tell from the way a single voice keeps talking that it's the news. But I can't hear anything else. I don't know whether both men are in the living room or just one.

Claudia shakes her head and fingers the necklace watch that hangs around her neck. Then she sits up tall and takes a sip of coffee. She sees me and her eyes get warm and soft. She smiles. *"Buon giorno,* Jackie." That means "good morning." I didn't do well figuring out Italian yesterday. But that's because I slept so poorly in the men's car the night before. I'll do better today.

Claudia goes to the counter and starts talking, just ordinary talking. It feels like she's talking to me, but she knows I can't understand. Well, that's good. If she talks a lot, I'll learn faster. I listen hard. Did she say the word *toast*? The English word?

She puts a slice of cheese and a slice of ham between two pieces of bread and then closes the sandwich into a thin metal basket that's obviously made to hold precisely one sandwich. She drops it into a toaster. Then she pours hot water from a teakettle into a cup and stirs it. She puts it on the table and gestures for me to sit down.

I sit and sniff the cup. It's hot chocolate. Hot chocolate on a summer morning. In Minnesota we drink hot chocolate only in the winter, but I love it. I'd drink it all year round if Mamma would make it.

Claudia stands by the toaster and talks as I drink my chocolate. She has her cup of coffee in her right hand, but her left hand moves in the air as she talks. I hear the word *buono* many times. And something that sounds like *allora.* But the words pass fast and I'm lost. She's chattering now, faster and faster, almost as though she can't stop herself. She takes the sandwich from the toaster and puts it on a plate in front of me.

The cheese has melted all around the ham. It's gooey and good. I've never had a sandwich for breakfast before, but I like it. And it's full of energy. I need energy today. I need to be ready for anything.

Claudia smiles as I eat. She looks happy. And she's still talking. Chattering.

The television turns off. I tense up, expecting the men to appear in the doorway from the living room. But now I hear the front door, the car engine.

I look quickly at Claudia, wondering if she'll try again to help me escape.

But Claudia avoids my eyes. She carries the plates to the sink, still talking. Then she turns to me and motions toward the third doorway of the kitchen, the only one I haven't gone through yet.

The knob on the door is made of wood, and it feels lovely under my hand, almost velvety. My uncle Jeb is a carpenter. He would love this doorknob.

I look back at Claudia to make sure this is what she meant. But she isn't even watching me. She's wiping off the table with a wet cloth. I turn the knob.

The small room has a washing machine and shelves of food in jars and cans and boxes.

And it has another door.

I open it. My breath catches. The world, the whole wide world, stretches out before me.

Claudia is beside me now. She talks again, gesturing toward the fields that I know the sea lies beyond. Then she shakes her finger no toward the direction of the dirt road. She makes a motor noise—like a truck—then a fearful grimace. I almost laugh, it's so much like you'd talk to a baby. But it's a lot nicer than the caveman grunts of the old man. And it works; I understand. She's warning me about that man in the truck. But she doesn't have to. I know he's bad. I'm old enough to understand that kind of bad. The very thought of him makes me queasy.

She takes the necklace watch off over her head and holds the face in front of me. Her finger taps on the number 1. She's still talking, but she's gesturing, too, and I know what she means. She puts the necklace over my head. It makes a little thump low on my chest.

I don't want to lie to Claudia. She's not like the men. But I can't promise to be back at one. I'm going to try to get to that town, at the bottom of the hill. I'm going home. So I look down at the watch and close my hand over it, not saying anything, not letting my eyes meet hers. She can think whatever she wants to think. But I have to do what I have to do.

Besides, she tried to help me get away yesterday. I

know she did. So maybe she even wants me to run away now. Letting me go outside on my own like this—she has to know that I'll run away. Anybody would know.

I go outside and hesitate. When I look back over my shoulder, Claudia's still standing there. But she doesn't look happy now. She seems tired—it's just morning, but her shoulders curve forward a little, like she's slumping, like yesterday when her father and brother found us out on the dirt road with the man in the truck.

She looks right at me and her eyes are sad. She closes the kitchen door.

I'm so confused. I can't figure her out. Why did she give me this watch if she knows I'll run away?

My mouth fills with her sadness. Maybe I do understand her. Maybe Claudia has decided to let whatever happens happen. She's given up.

I'm on my own.

But what if I'm wrong? What if she's watching from the window to see what I do?

All right, I'll play it careful. I walk in the direction that she gestured, through the pines. There's a clear path. Once I'm past the pine grove, the ground turns to stone rubble, and I can see the water beyond. The sea. It's creamy green. I stand there, checking the watch. After fifteen minutes, I turn around and run in the direction of the road. But I don't take the path—I don't want to go too close to the house again. I cut off through the grasses.

A snake slithers past in front of me.

I almost scream.

It's the same kind I saw on the steps with Claudia. Are they everywhere? This is so unfair. If only it weren't snakes—snakes of all things. Nothing could be worse.

I'm standing with one foot on top of the other, shaking and straining my eyes to see what's in the grass all around. I think I hear them, slip, slip, slip, cold and crawling.

I can't do this. I can't go through the grass. I just can't.

I turn around carefully, scanning the grasses for snakes. I stomp in place. Snakes are deaf—I learned that from the airplane magazine. But they feel vibrations in the ground. That's usually how they find their prey. But most snakes will go away if they sense something big coming.

The ground becomes stony just a little ahead, where I was a moment ago. It will be easy to spot a snake. I can get there. I have to. I force myself to take a step. And now I'm running. And there's no grass anymore, so I'm just running. Away, away.

The air is full of the smell of salt water. I race and stop short. The hill crests and drops off as though some giant has split it apart. I'm so startled, I feel unsteady, like I could lose my footing and plunge to my death. I sit down and hug myself till the feeling passes. Small waves lap around rocks that stick out of the water close to the shore.

A little way off to the right, a thin strip of sand lines a wide cove. Small, long-legged birds walk on the beach. Nothing feels like Minnesota.

My watch says it's almost ten o'clock. There's no road anywhere in sight over here. I should turn around and take the path back to the dirt road and stop a car. If I hear a truck coming—that old blue truck—I can hide in the grapevines.

If I'm fast enough.

My mouth goes wet and sour with fear.

Plus Claudia's father or brother or both are out somewhere in the car. If they came along that road and saw me, they'd take me right to the house. And they'd be angry.

And Claudia has given up. Claudia won't fight for me anymore.

I could take the steps down the hillside. Except for the snakes.

I sit with my knees cocked upward and wrap my arms around them. The scabs on my knees pull tight, so I lick them to soften them a little and make them not hurt. Then I tuck my head under, with my forehead on my knees. This way I'm as small as I can be. But I feel even smaller. I feel like no one.

Well, that's no way to feel. If Mamma were here, she'd tell me to buck up. That's what she says: "Buck up, Jackie." Those words always give me courage. I stand and spread my legs and arms out far and turn in a slow circle, taking up all the room I possibly can.

I talk out loud. "My name is Jackie Holt. Jacqueline Holt, really. But I like to be called Jackie because it seems less fancy, more like who I really am. I live at 24 Silvan Lane in St. Cloud, Minnesota. I have a Social Security number, but I never learned it. I think it starts with 9, though. My favorite color is green. My favorite number is 17. My favorite letter is J. That's not because of my name, it's because of my dog's name—Jersey. And I don't really know why my favorite number is 17. It just is. And no one asks why my favorite color is green. I guess that's because lots of people like green. I can swim good. And I'm an excellent reader. My favorite subjects are science and math. I read science books all the time. In September I'll be in sixth grade. I don't have any brothers or sisters, but I have two cousins who live in my town and three more who live in New Jersey. That's why my dog is named Jersey—my cousin Eddie helped me buy him when we were visiting them one year.

"My cousins love me. And so do my aunts and uncles. And my grandparents—all four of them. And Noëlle, my best friend. And probably Sarah; she used to be my best friend. And Mrs. Wilcox, my old teacher from third grade. She told us she loved all of us, and I believe her.

"And Mamma loves me." My voice catches. But I won't let myself cry, especially not now when I'm trying so hard to be strong. "Mamma loves me," I say again, louder. That's why I can't shrink down to no one. That's why I have to get home again.

But Mamma wouldn't want me to walk on the dirt road when those men are out there. And Mamma wouldn't want me to go through the grass or down the steps when snakes are hiding.

Mamma would say, "Why, Jackie, you can't even speak the language. Be practical. Find someone to help you." That's what she'd say, isn't it? Find someone you can trust.

Like Claudia.

Claudia might not be ready to fight for me anymore, but that doesn't mean she won't help me. I bet she'll help me. I know she's good. She hasn't done anything wrong, after all. Even when she told me not to go toward the road, she wasn't being bad. She was just warning about the man. She was protecting me. She is good. I trust her.

I have to trust someone.

"Mamma," I whisper now, "Mamma. Forgive me for hating snakes. Forgive me for being afraid of the strange people around here. I'll come back to you. I just can't go down the road on my own. I can't. I'm sorry. I'm so sorry, Mamma."

8

I t isn't hard to find the steps cut into the side of the cliff going down to the beach. I knew they'd be there. If someone took the effort to make steps down the hill to the paved road below, then this whole countryside is probably full of steps that lead to all sorts of places. And a beach, well, anyone would want to have steps down to a beach.

They're steep—a lot steeper than the steps Claudia took me on yesterday. Some of the steps are at least three or four times deeper from one step to the next as ordinary stairs are. A little kid could never climb down them alone. I'm lucky my legs are long. And now I'm grateful these clothes are just a little bit loose on me. It makes it easier to move.

By the time I reach the bottom, I'm slathered in sweat. Even my hair is damp. I take off my sneakers, and the sand scorches the bottom of my feet. I leave the sneakers on the last step and run to the edge of the water. It sweeps up around me, cool and welcome. I walk in water up to my ankles. Little white crabs scurry across the sand, in and out of the water. I'm careful not to step on them. I'm not too afraid of crabs, they're not like snakes. Even the lakes back home have lots of crabs at the edges. But the way they move so fast makes me skittish.

The long-legged birds quickly move far away from me. But not so far that I can't see everything they do. I watch one pick up a crab in its beak, throw back its head, and open its beak to swallow the crab whole. I imagine a tiny crab pinching the inside of the bird's throat and stomach. But stomach acids probably kill it fast.

The water makes little sucking noises at the rocks and slapping noises on the sand. I can't hear anything else. My heartbeat speeds up and I feel lost again. But it's not so bad this time. Nothing on this beach seems threatening.

I walk slowly the full length of the cove, watching the birds scatter ahead of me.

A few plants grow out of the sides of the cliff surrounding this cove from about five or six feet up all the way to the top. Prickly plants. I didn't take a close look at them as I was climbing down the steps. So now I leave the water and run across the hot sand to the cliff. It doesn't burn as much as before, because the beach is narrower here and partly shaded. I stand at the bottom and look straight up. They're raspberry canes. But I don't see any berries. How funny. I didn't know raspberries could grow out of rock.

At home the raspberries are ripening. There are tons of them down by the stream behind Noëlle's house. Mamma and Noëlle's mother are friends. Mamma said she'd pick lots of raspberries and stick them in the freezer for me to eat over ice cream when I come home. When I come home.

I put one hand inside the other and make a ball and press them against my stomach to stop that sick feeling. I will make it home. I can't let myself think anything else. If I do, I'll get so sad and slow I won't see the opportunities for escape. I can't think about Mamma.

And, oh, I can't think about Daddy at all.

When the sick feeling passes, I look up again and examine the whole cliff. The bottom five or six feet, the parts where plants don't grow, are darker here in the shade than they are out in the sun. I touch the side of the cliff. It's damp. And there are bits of seaweed stuck here and there, even in the parts in full sunlight. I understand: at high tide the beach disappears and the water comes up over my head.

I look back to the steps I came down, way on the other end of the cove. Only the bottom ones show from here, because the others are almost entirely hidden by the cliff plants. I've been walking on the beach maybe a half hour or so. It couldn't have been longer than that—I really don't think so. So it'll take only thirty minutes to get back to the steps. The tide can't come in that fast, can it? I don't have experience with tides.

I'm not taking any chances. I go back to the water and now I'm running, splashing the water up my shins, practically stumbling as I try to avoid the crabs. It's silly. The water won't swallow me and I can swim, anyway. But I can't help it. Panic makes me stupid.

By the time I arrive at the foot of the steps, I'm out of breath. But my body won't stop. I'm climbing the steps, holding on to the scrub brush that grows out of the side of the cliff here—some sort of shiny vine, not just raspberries.

Halfway up, I finally stop and clear off a step enough to collapse on it. I look out at the sea. If the tide has come in any, I can't tell. But I'm safe here.

I sit like that till my heart is beating normally again.

My watch says five minutes after twelve. How did that happen?

I better start back.

If something happens along the way, if I see an opportunity for escape, I'll make a run for it. But if not, I'll go back. Maybe after lunch I'll have the energy to figure out something.

I get up to continue climbing when I see a smooth, egg-shaped rock on the side of the next step up, pushed into the dirt and stone of the cliff. I didn't notice it on my way down the steps before. All the other rocks are jagged and randomly shaped. This one is remarkable.

It's lodged pretty tight, so I have to work it side to side to get it free. It isn't an ordinary rock, after all. It's one of those geodes. I've seen them before, in the natural history museum in Minneapolis. I don't own one, but some of the other kids in my school do. You can buy them in the museum store. They're oval rocks, normal looking on the outside—except for their shape—but inside they're special. Inside they have beautiful crystals that form sharp spikes, like glass.

This one is broken open, and the crystals inside are purple. It looks like amethyst to me.

Something's stuck down between the spikes of the crystals. A shell of some sort. Maybe a crab. I fit the edges together again carefully and clean off the outside. My hands cradle it.

I climb the rest of the way up the steps. When I reach the top, I spy a stand of trees not too far away. I run to the closest one.

Green berries stick out of the tree everywhere, sort of like cherries. We have plenty of cherry trees in St. Cloud, so I know them. Cherry trees have speckled bark, not gnarly bark like these trees. I stand directly under a group of berries and squint up at them. Oh, I think they're olives, that's what I think they are. Olives. I look around. These trees go on and on in neatly planted rows. I'm at the edge of an olive grove.

I wonder who this land belongs to. A twinge of fear makes me pause. I don't want to meet any more strange people. Especially not people who think I'm trespassing on their land. Daddy may have thought southerners were friendly, but he didn't know people like the man in the blue truck. I'm sure of that.

Still, I can't leave yet; I came here for a reason. I break a small twig from the tree—a perfect twig for the job—and run back to the edge of the cliff, clutching the geode to my chest. I poke around in the crystals. Then I shake the geode, open side down.

A claw falls in my hand. But not a crab claw. It's one of those tiny plastic claws for your hair. It's pearly colored. And it has a bird on it—a lovely rose-colored bird. The back of my neck goes prickly, all the way up to my ears.

I have butterfly hair claws at home. And fairy ones, too. But this one is prettier than any of mine. I feel almost like it's a gift, something miniature and perfect waiting here just for me. Like a message. A secret special message. Lucky.

My shorts have a small pocket in the rear on the right side. I slip the pearl claw in and make sure it goes all the way to the bottom, so it can't fall out.

Immediately I feel like a thief. Even though I don't know who it belongs to. And even if someone purposely hid her hair claw in the geode, she must have forgotten about it, because the geode was stuck in the dirt, as though it had been like that for a long time. Plus, the steps are so grown over with vines that I bet no one's climbed them in a while. So taking the hair claw isn't a bad thing.

And a hair claw isn't worth anything.

But a geode is. I don't remember how much they cost, but I know it's several dollars.

I climb down the steps halfway and replace the geode, pressing it hard into its spot.

I head back toward the white house. When it comes in sight, I move more quickly. And now I can see Claudia at the door. She's wearing a blue dress and her hair is in a ponytail, and she's watching. Watching for me. And even though I don't want to feel this way, I'm a little glad that she's there. It's nice the way she's watching. Familiar. Something familiar in this foreign world.

She smiles at me—a wide, genuine smile. Claudia is happy to see me.

I run to her.

⑨

We ate a lunch of tomato salad and bread and lots of cold grapes. Just the two of us. We cleaned up together. And now we sit side by side at the table again, Claudia and me. She put a giant chopping board down. It's so big that both of us can chop at the same time. She's doing carrots. I'm doing celery. We're preparing tonight's dinner, I'm sure.

At home we don't cook much. We get take-out Chinese or pizza. Or we eat prepared foods that just pop in the microwave for a few minutes and come out great. We set the table together and clean up together, but it isn't like working together making a meal. So this is new.

The funny thing is, I really like it. I like helping in the kitchen. And Claudia even lets me use the big knife. When she handed it to me, it felt strange. Heavy. And the blade looked sharper than any of the knives we have at home. I didn't begin right away, because I felt so unsure. I just held the knife and watched her.

She slit the carrots lengthwise several times. Then she lined up all the long pieces, and now she's chopping them into tiny cubes. So I'm doing the same thing to the celery. My cubes aren't as regular as Claudia's. They vary a lot in size. But she hasn't criticized them. In fact, she hasn't even really looked at them. It's as though she just trusts me to do a good job. So I'm trying hard.

Vegetables are good food. Adults who don't know me are usually surprised when I eat all mine. Like the businessmen who took Daddy and me to lunch. They kept saying what a good girl I was. Most of my friends really like vegetables, too. But we eat the prepared kind. Or, sometimes, the frozen kind. These are fresh. This will be a really good dinner, I bet.

At the last dinner I had with Daddy in the restaurant, we ate asparagus. They were covered with olive oil and salt, and when the waiter put them on the table, he squeezed lemon juice over them right in front of us. Daddy said he loved asparagus, and he served me a big helping. He said I'd love them, too. And I did.

Now I'm getting sad again. And my heart's quickening in that crazy way it's been doing all day.

So I sing. I don't sing words, because Claudia doesn't

know English, and I don't want her to feel left out. So I just sing lots of la-la-la's to melodies I like.

After a while Claudia joins in. But she doesn't know the melodies and that ruins it. Still, I think I'm okay now. I can concentrate on chopping. I stop singing. Claudia looks over at me, but I don't answer her face. I stay busy with the celery.

When we finish, she washes three big tomatoes. She uses soap, like the young man did last night. Then she slices one and puts it in front of me. She takes away my knife and hands me a new knife. It's the weirdest knife I've ever seen. The blade is arched, like a part of a circle. And there are handles on both ends. I examine it from every side.

Claudia smiles at me. She takes back the knife and holds it by both handles. The knife curves downward between her hands, like a capital C that fell on its back. She places the lowest point of the curve on the slice of tomato, then rocks it from side to side. The knife chops up the tomato, all tiny in crazy shapes.

I laugh.

Claudia smiles wider and hands the rocking knife back to me. *"Forza,"* she says. A word of encouragement. I like it. *Forza.* Like Mamma saying, "Buck up."

I rock away, cutting up tomato slices. It doesn't take long to finish all three tomatoes.

A car engine comes close, sputters, and stops. I recognize that engine now. I look at Claudia.

She cuts a head of cabbage in half and slices it, then puts the slices in front of me. She looks at me expectantly. How can she do that? How can she just pretend her father and brother don't exist?

The brother comes in. He says something and drops a newspaper on the table.

There's a photograph of Daddy on the front page. I grab the paper. Everything else about me is rigid, but my hands shake. Claudia tries to take the newspaper from me. I won't let her. I have to look at Daddy's picture. What does it say? Oh, what does it say?

Claudia folds me into her arms, the newspaper crushed between us. I won't yield to her body. I hold myself stiff. She pushes the cutting board and all the vegetables aside. She talks gently and helps me spread out the paper on the table. I kneel on my chair so I can see everything better.

Below Daddy's photograph, there are two photographs of me. One is my fifth-grade school picture. The other is my passport picture. Neither of them is any good. My hair was long in the school picture, because I didn't cut it until December vacation. And I've got a funny look on my face in the passport picture. How could anyone recognize me from these?

I look at Claudia. "What does it say?"

Claudia's reading. Every now and then she says something to the man. He mumbles a word or two, and she goes on reading.

"What does it say?" I want to shout at her, but she can't answer me anyway, not in words I can understand. I'm itchy all over, itchy and wired. That's what Daddy calls it when I can't sit still. I've never been this wired before.

Claudia looks at her brother. "Oh, Francesco," she says. She puts her hand over her mouth and sits back.

I flinch. Her brother's name is Francesco. I didn't want to know his name. I won't let it come in my head. I'll call him her brother. I refuse to know him.

Claudia's brother sets a glass on the table and drops in a few ice cubes. He goes into the little storage room, where the door to the outside is, and comes back with a large, wide bottle. He pours reddish liquid into the glass, filling it halfway. I know the odor: wine. Then he gets a bottle of fizzy water from the refrigerator and fills the glass the rest of the way. He puts both hands on the table as he lowers himself into a chair, and he drinks.

They talk to each other in a tired way. Claudia shakes her head a lot. Her brother drinks.

"Please tell me. Try to tell me. What does it say? About Daddy . . . what does it say?"

Claudia holds her hands out and shrugs in apology. She keeps shaking her head.

I bend over the newspaper again. I examine the words. Nothing looks familiar. There's Daddy's name. And Minnesota. And the words *americano* and *polizia* and *abbandonato*. But nothing else holds any meaning for me. I don't see Mamma's name anywhere. But they give my name under my passport photo.

My head is buzzing. Daddy was limp and his skin changed and he felt cooler. Daddy was cooler and now he's on the front page of the newspaper and he was cooler and I know what that means and he was cooler. And my head is buzzing. The buzzing is so loud, I can hardly stay upright. I lie down on the floor.

Claudia's kneeling over me, saying things with so much worry on her face. She's ordering her brother around. And he looks scared, too. He hands her something small and white.

I like this buzzing. I want it to keep up. I don't want to hear them talk. I can't understand them anyway.

Claudia holds the white thing under my nose.

The sharp stink of garlic makes the inside of my nose sting. My eyes hurt, too. I turn my head away, but Claudia moves the thing with me. I shake my head, more and more, and now I'm shaking my head violently from side to side and I'm kicking my feet and I don't know what I'm doing, I'm just screaming and nothing matters but the buzzing and the screaming.

That's all there is, all there is in the whole world, one huge scream.

Claudia has pulled me to her again, and I'm sitting on her lap on the floor. I'm not moving anymore. I'm exhausted.

Claudia strokes my back and talks to the man. He's writing down things as she talks. A column of words. A list maybe.

I watch what they do, but I don't feel anything. I'm too tired to feel anything. I guess that's what they call a tantrum, what just happened to me.

Mamma likes to say I was an easy baby. I never had tantrums. What would she think now? A moment ago I lay on the floor like a two-year-old, flailing about.

But I'm not even ashamed of myself. I'm too tired. And I don't care what the man thinks. I don't even care what Claudia thinks of me. I won't look at their faces. I don't want to know what they think.

Claudia's hugging me still, and rocking her torso backward and forward. It feels good.

"You can stop now," I say at last. "I won't do it again." I push away from her and stand up.

The man looks at me. He folds the little piece of paper he's been writing on and stuffs it in his pocket. Then he takes the newspaper and goes into the living room.

Claudia stands, too. She looks at the vegetables on the table and lets out a loud sigh. She gets an onion from a bin under the counter and peels it.

I don't want to just go on making dinner. Claudia can pretend nothing's wrong, but I won't. I go through the little storage room and out the back door.

Claudia comes after me, but she doesn't try to stop me. She calls over her shoulder to her brother, something long and complicated, and comes to stand by my side. She waits.

I don't know which way to go. With Claudia beside me, I could face the steps down the hill again, despite the snakes. Or we could go on the dirt road.

Her brother's at the door now. If he touches me, I'll bolt. I'll run for the road. He says something. Then he disappears inside.

"*Vieni.*" Claudia walks in big strides, the same direction I went this morning.

I follow her. It's not really like I have a choice, anyway.

Before she gets to the cliff, she turns and goes straight for the olive grove. She walks fast, and I have to practically run to keep up with her.

On the other side of the grove, there's a wild area, with lots of pine trees. The rocks and undergrowth make it harder to walk and we're clearly going uphill, but Claudia doesn't slow down. If anything, she speeds up. She doesn't seem the least bit concerned about snakes. I stay right behind her, stepping in her footsteps.

There are lots of types of trees now, most of them skinny and tall. The only ones I recognize are beech, because of their smooth bark and the way their leaves stand out flat to the sun, keeping the light away from the ground, so there's very little undergrowth in beech groves. But the sunlight sneaks down around the other trees in streaks here and there. The noises of the woods are all quiet noises, wind and birds. Like it must have been a hundred years ago. A thousand years ago even. I feel like we've gone backward in time. Like I'm a pioneer girl. Or Little Red Riding Hood. I look around, warily.

We come out on a trail. It's narrow and windy and full of rocks, but it's definitely a trail. I'm hopeful again. If there's a trail, then it connects people.

I can hear something, something like singing. We come out at a stream that's rushing along toward the sea. A bridge made of two parallel poles, with split logs going across them, spans the stream. It's high up—at least a six- or seven-foot drop. And the bridge must be three times that in length.

Claudia stops and sits on a boulder beside this end of the bridge. She says something to me. And she looks around, as though she's totally distracted.

Am I supposed to go across? On my own? It doesn't look sturdy.

I walk over to Claudia and tap her on the knee. When she doesn't respond, I shake her knee.

Claudia blinks at me, as though she's waking up. She stands and walks across the bridge, just like that, without hesitating. Maybe she's done it a thousand times before.

I walk across slowly. Some of the split logs shift under my feet, and my stomach lurches. But I get to the other side safely. Now what?

The trail continues through the woods, but Claudia's off the trail, kicking through the leaves and pine needles on the ground. She stoops and picks something, then holds it up to show me. A mushroom. She goes on picking mushrooms.

I follow the trail alone.

Claudia calls to me. She says, "No," another word I understand.

No. No what? No, I shouldn't go this way. But why? Because the people at the other end of this trail will help me—or because they won't? Which is it? Who can I trust?

The buzzing starts in my head again. Everything is awful. Everything is too too awful. I sit down, right there in the dirt of the trail.

Claudia picks more mushrooms, holding them in the scoop of her skirt. She pauses often, standing silent, as though nothing in the world could ever rush her. When she finally comes to me and says, *"Vieni,"* I'm surprised. It's as though I thought she'd go on picking mushrooms forever.

We walk back, with her talking now, pointing at birds, saying things about them as though I should care.

The whole time I'm wondering why I didn't run away when she was picking the mushrooms, why I'm not running away now—just bolting over that bridge, along that trail to wherever it leads. I'm wondering why I'm more afraid of what's out there than what's back in the white house, why I'm acting like such a little kid.

⑩

We were gone a long time. Long enough that Claudia's brother finished making dinner. He's stirring a pot on the stove when we come in, and he acts so nice, like he's really glad to see us, like he wants us to be happy. And not just Claudia. Oh, it's clear he loves Claudia. But now he wants me to be happy, too. He says something light and cheery to me.

Is he an idiot? Or is it that he thinks I'm an idiot? No smiles can change what he did, what he's doing. I look away.

The table is set with soup bowls, four of them, and there's a wooden bowl with a hunk of white cheese in it and a cheese grater in the center of the table. A long loaf of bread sits on a cutting board with a knife resting beside it.

Claudia puts a cold bottle of fizzy water on the table

and that large bottle of wine. She takes a carton of milk out of the refrigerator and asks me something.

I recognize the word for "American" again, but that carton doesn't look American to me. I shake my head. American kids like to drink milk, sure, but not Italian milk. Italian milk is gross.

Daddy said it was okay to go three weeks without milk. He said my teeth won't rot in that amount of time. And I won't even be in Italy three weeks, after all. Because I'm going home. I'm going home as soon as I can get to a phone and call the *polizia*.

Claudia calls out toward the living room. Then she sits and motions for me to sit, too. So I do.

Claudia's father comes in. This is the first time I've seen him today. I wonder where he's been. He unbuttons his shirt and folds it neatly over the back of a chair. His undershirt is white and sleeveless, and black chest hair shows over the scooped neck—black, even though his head hair is gray. He smooths the shirt again. And I get it: it's his work clothes. The old man has a job. He drops into the chair and slaps his hands on his thighs. The chair legs scrape noisily on the floor as he moves it forward. He rests both arms on the table on either side of his bowl. Finally, he looks at me. His eyes are steady. I can't see anything in them—no meanness, no craziness, nothing. I look right back at him, holding my eyes as steady as I can. At least he doesn't give a great big happy smile—not like his son.

The son says something to the father. Then he ladles soup into the bowls. Soup. That's what Claudia and I were chopping vegetables for before—soup. I'm surprised, like I was when Claudia made me the hot chocolate this morning. At home we eat soup in the winter, when it's freezing out. The steam in my face always makes me feel safe, like I've conquered the weather and nothing can ever freeze my toes. But now it's hot out. Even as the light fades, it's hot.

The soup smells great, though, I have to admit it. I know this soup. It comes in a can at home. I like it. It's minestrone. But in the can the vegetables aren't cut up nearly as small as Claudia and I cut them. And there are tiny shell-shaped noodles in this soup. They're cute.

The son sits down and says, *"Buon appetito."* I know those words, too, because every businessman Daddy and I had lunch with started the meal with those words. It means you should have a good meal. Sort of like a really short blessing. I wonder why they didn't say it at dinner last night. I guess that makeshift meal of tomatoes and cheese didn't count.

The old man and Claudia repeat, *"Buon appetito."*

I blow on a big spoonful of carrots and baby lima beans and those noodles. Then I eat it. And it's good.

Really good. So much better than the cans. I didn't want to like it—I didn't want to like anything the son made. But I'm eating in spite of myself. And, anyway, Claudia and I cut most of these vegetables, so it's not all the son's doing.

Claudia grates cheese onto the top of her soup, then offers it to me. But the soup is just right as it is. I shake my head. She motions for me to pass the cheese across the table, to the son. But I don't want to. It's enough that I'm eating the soup he made. I don't want to have anything else to do with him. I pretend not to understand.

The son looks at me, and his eyes go liquid. They seem to plead. He knows what I'm doing. For an instant I almost feel sorry for him. I'm just about to give in and pass him the cheese when he reaches far out and takes it. He grates a lot into his soup and passes the cheese to his father. Everyone eats with concentration.

At home we talk all through dinner. And even when I was traveling alone with Daddy, the two of us talked all the time. But dinner was silent last night. And now this dinner is silent, too. I wonder if that's just because I'm here.

I'm glad, though. I wouldn't understand anything if they did talk. And I want to eat my soup. And I don't want to like these men.

When we finish, the father and son talk to each

other. Claudia intervenes, but I can tell that the father is insisting on something. He says, *"Vieni,"* so many times. Finally, the brother gets up and the men leave. They go outside, and I hear the car drive away.

Claudia and I clean up.

She picks up a bag off the counter. I saw it when we came in before dinner. She says, *"Vieni,"* what feels like the constant refrain by now, and we go out the door into the corridor that leads to the bathroom.

Claudia passes the bathroom and opens the next door down.

Birds chirp noisily.

I step inside, behind Claudia. It's dark in here and cooler, like in the living room. And now I can see cages of little birds. Five cages in all. They hang at my face level from metal stands.

Claudia puts the bag on the floor and pulls on a wide strap. The shutters go up, clacking loudly. The windows are already halfway open. But she opens them fully now—all three of them. And she attaches a metal rod to a clip on the bottom slat of the shutters, so that it sticks out the window. She does this to each window. Then she takes one of the birdcages and hangs it from one of those metal rods, so that it's swinging gently outside the window. The bird chirps change to singing immediately.

I've already unhooked another cage from its stand

and I hand it to Claudia. We work together until all the cages hang outside, one at one window and two at the others.

The birds sing riotously. This must be the high point of their day. They're tiny and I'm pretty sure they're finches, because they come in lots of colors. And one cage has parakeets in greens and blues. Anyone can recognize that kind of bird.

The room feels larger now that the birds are hanging outside. On one wall there's a crucifix—Jesus nailed to a cross—above a single bed. The bedsheets have beautiful tropical fish on them.

The toy cat that the men took from Daddy's rental car sits on the pillow along with the nightgown I wore last night. I suck my breath in. This must mean I'm supposed to sleep here tonight—not in Claudia's room. I'm confused. It was strange to sleep on one half of Claudia's bed, but somehow changing to another room feels even stranger. It definitely means I'll be alone all night.

I go over to the bed and pick up the toy cat. It's been washed, and its fur stands out all fluffy. That was nice of Claudia. I give her a quick smile.

On every wall there are photographs with a girl in them. This must be her room—that girl whose clothes I'm wearing. "Where is she?" I ask, pointing at one of the biggest photographs.

Claudia folds her arms across her chest and watches me.

Against the wall opposite to the bed there's a desk and a set of drawers and a big basket full of stuffed animals. Against a third wall there's a bookcase with books on the top two shelves and dolls on the bottom two shelves.

I look at the books. None of the covers are familiar. I pick one up at random and open it. On the copyright page in tiny letters are the English words *Island of the Blue Dolphin*. So this is the translation. I've read that book. I liked it a lot. I close the book and open another, but there's no English on the copyright page of this one.

The son comes into the room. The birds are so loud, I didn't even hear the car come back. He says something brief to Claudia, as though he just wants her to know he's back. Then he goes away. I hear the loud burst of television voices from the living room.

Claudia says something and points with a little motion of her chin toward the direction of the living room. That's exactly what her father did yesterday—that same chin pointing. She's asking me if I want to watch television. I shake my head and hold the book to my chest.

Claudia asks something I don't understand. Then she takes the book from me, turns on a standing lamp, and sits on the bed. She taps a spot beside her. So I sit down.

And she reads to me. She reads just like she told me stories yesterday at nap time and last night, before I went to sleep.

Lots of kids are embarrassed to be read to when they're my age. They think it's silly when you already know how to read. And, I have to admit, it is slower. Reading silently is fast. But I don't care; I like to be read to. Mamma reads to me every night. And the only really bad part about our trip to Italy before two nights ago was that I forgot to bring a book for Daddy to read to me. I brought one that I was reading to myself—*Watership Down*. It's a book all about rabbits, so even though the story isn't true, I get to learn a lot that is true, anyway. It's a fat book, and it's hard, so I didn't have to bring any others—I knew I wouldn't even finish that one. Still, I should have brought some other book for Daddy to read to me, just a chapter a day or something.

Claudia is a good reader. Her voice goes up and down, and she acts surprised at times and excited at times. I wonder if she's a teacher. Besides Mamma, teachers are the best out-loud readers. At least among the adults I know. Old Mrs. Stevens, across the street back home, baby-sits for me when we can't get a college student to come. And she likes to read to me, but she's terrible. I try to act like I'm interested, but really my mind goes off everywhere else when Mrs. Stevens reads.

But I'm listening now to Claudia, which is really weird, since I don't even know what she's saying.

She reads to the end of the chapter. Then she folds the book jacket flap into the pages, as a marker, and puts the book flat on the desk.

She picks up the bag from the floor and takes out a pair of sneakers. They're brand-new. She puts one on the floor and nestles it up beside my foot and talks. The new sneaker is a little bigger than the one on my foot. So she knew that these sneakers were small on me. She must have measured them against my patent-leather shoes. She must have told her brother to go buy sneakers while we were out in the woods before dinner. Maybe that's one of the things he was writing on that piece of paper—my shoe size.

"I don't want new sneakers," I say. My hands shake, but I won't let myself go crazy again—I won't have a tantrum. I try to slow my breathing. "I want my patent-leather shoes back. Please."

Claudia reaches into the bag again. She hands me a new toothbrush. Her face is calm. She takes a hairbrush out of the bag. And a stack of new underpants. And a few pairs of socks—white ones that are woven in pretty designs. And a pair of sunglasses, pink with sparkles. Her eyes don't meet mine.

So she's doing it to me now. She's acting like nothing is wrong, like she does with her father and brother.

She's changed. Something made Claudia change her mind. Before, she tried to console me when I acted miserable. But not now.

I look at the things she told her brother to buy. She's acting like I'm going to be here a long time.

My whole body trembles.

I pick up the sneaker on the floor and I run to the closest window. I throw it as far as I can.

⑪

The birds give off a slightly sweet odor. They make snuffly noises as they snuggle against each other in sleep. The house is quiet, though. Our house in Minnesota creaks and groans all night. Daddy says it's because the pipes are old.

I'm lying in the dark, the pitch black. No streetlight comes in through the windows—because there are no streets, of course. But there's not even a hint of moonlight. The moon must be blocked by the thick pine trees.

It's good to have clean teeth finally. And my bath was sweet bubbles again. And I love this nightgown. But they can't change my mind. This isn't right; this isn't my life.

And the girl whose room this is will get mad at them when she comes home and sees what they've done. I'd be mad at Mamma if she took someone, just snatched her off the street, and put her in my room. But Mamma would never do that. No one decent would do that.

Claudia's father and brother took me. I don't know why, but it doesn't matter why. They're wrong.

Tears run out of the corners of my eyes, down my temples, into my ears. They stole me. As though I'm not real. As though I'm a doll or something.

The girl whose room this is has two dolls in the basket with the stuffed animals. Barbie dolls. I didn't know they sold Barbie in Italy.

But I didn't find anything else American. I looked through every book before I went to bed. There's nothing in English.

I wanted to look through the drawers, but I wouldn't like it if someone looked through my drawers at home without asking me. So I just talked to the birds for a long time. Then Claudia came back and brought the birds in and shut the windows partway. She took a pair of shorts and a shirt out of the drawers and set them on top of the bureau, then kissed me on the forehead.

Maybe she's crazy. Like the men.

And maybe I am, too, because I felt sort of grateful for that kiss. It should have turned my stomach.

After she left I walked around the room looking at the photos. They're all pictures of this girl growing up.

She's my age, I'm sure, because there are no photos of her older than about ten or eleven. Claudia's with her lots of the time. And in one photo Claudia's mother and father stand on either side of Claudia and a man. The girl is in the very middle. She was smaller then—no more than five. The man is obviously Claudia's husband. And the girl is her daughter.

Claudia's husband must be traveling somewhere with her daughter. Like I went traveling with Daddy. A shiver shoots up my spine. I don't want to think about this anymore.

And maybe I don't like this girl so much. It's stuck-up to have photos of yourself all over your walls.

From outside comes a creak of tree branches in the wind.

This house is far away from anything I know.

Suddenly I remember. I get up and go to the bureau, where I folded my dirty clothes. I take the little pearly hair claw out of the shorts pocket and put it under my pillow. It's silly, but the hair claw makes me feel strong now. Claudia and her father and brother don't know about it. It's my secret. I have control over it.

I climb back in bed, roll on my side, and close my eyes. Sleep is important. Daddy says you can't make good decisions if you don't get enough sleep. And I have to make good decisions.

The birds wake me. I can tell it's really early from the light and just the feel of the air. I put on a pair of the new underwear and the shorts and shirt Claudia set out for me last night. I slip the little hair claw into the back pocket of these shorts, and I go out into the corridor and to the bathroom. Then I walk quietly through the kitchen.

I've taken a few steps into the living room before I notice that the son is sleeping on the couch. Doesn't he live here? The way they all eat together, I just assumed they lived together. Maybe he's sleeping on the couch to make sure I can't sneak out.

I won't take the chance of waking him.

I back out of the living room and tiptoe fast to my bedroom. No, it's not my bedroom. It's just the one I slept in.

It's stupid to think of going anywhere without shoes. One sneaker remains in the bag. The other one is off somewhere in the dirt outside.

I put a pair of the socks in my back pocket, on top of the hair claw. Then I open a window wide and consider the jump. It's far enough to break a leg. That wouldn't be so bad, though, because then they'd have to take me to a doctor, and a doctor would listen to me; a doctor would help me. I drop the one new sneaker out the window, and I hoist myself up so that I'm balanced on the window ledge on my stomach, with my legs hanging back into the room. The metal rails that frame the window dig into my belly. I put one foot up beside my stomach and lift myself onto my hands. Now I'm perched there, on two hands and one foot. The other foot still hangs behind in the room. But it's scary like this. I feel like I'm going to fall out onto my head. Plus the rail really hurts my hands. So I get back down on my stomach and wiggle and twist, even though the rail digs in like mad, until I've turned myself around. I'm still balancing on my stomach, but my legs hang out the window now and my head sticks into the room.

It's now or never.

I grip the inside lip of the window ledge and push myself backward. The rail hits me across my forearms now. It hurts awful. I let go.

I land on my feet with a *whop* and fall back on my bottom. My hands slam into the dirt. They sting. And my bottom aches. But I'm okay.

I grab the sneaker and go looking for the other one, stomping the ground as I go, to scare off snakes. I know I threw it in this direction, but I can't find it anywhere. What a dumb thing I did.

"Jackie."

Claudia comes from the back door. She's still wearing her nightgown, like yesterday morning. In her hand is the other sneaker, the one I've been looking for.

I sit on the ground and wipe off the bottom of my feet and put on the sneakers and socks. I don't even say anything. What's the point? Part of me feels defeated. But part of me feels relief. I don't want to risk breaking bones. And I don't want to go wandering off all alone. I need someone to help me.

Claudia leads me by the hand and we go inside, into the kitchen. She motions me to sit at the table and she says something, nodding her head, as though she wants me to agree with her.

She opens the refrigerator and takes out a plastic bag. Then she sprinkles flour on the table and drops a lump of dough from the bag onto the floury spot. She presses it flat with her hands.

It smells yeasty. We have a German bakery in downtown St. Cloud, my hometown, which smells like that. On Sunday mornings Mamma and Daddy and I drive there and we buy a little box of treats. Then we go on up to Glenwood, where Grandma and Grandpa live, and we all eat cinnamon buns and gingerbread and pound cake and so many good things.

I should feel sad, thinking about my family, and I do, way down deep inside, but I'm also fascinated. I've never seen anyone do this sort of cooking.

Claudia opens a low cupboard and takes out a rolling pin. She hands it to me.

The rolling pin is really heavy—a lot heavier than that rocking knife yesterday. It's made of some kind of stone—maybe even marble. Daddy and I visited a marble quarry north of Rome, so I know that Italy has a big marble industry. The rolling part twirls easily on a wooden stick through its center. I can imagine Daddy admiring it.

Claudia's watching me. I see her out of the corner of my eye. She's trying to lure me with this rolling pin. She could see how much I enjoyed helping her cook yesterday, so she wants to use that now. She wants me to forget about jumping out of windows and running away.

People think that kids don't know anything about manipulation. Boy, are they wrong. I don't hate teachers who manipulate us. Or librarians. Or school bus drivers. I'm used to it. They're usually doing it because they need us to be someplace on time or to act better. It's for our own good. Usually. At least, that's what I think. But Claudia's not doing it for my own good.

The terrible thing is, I want to roll the dough. It would be fun. I want to see what we're going to make.

If I'm doing it because I want to do it, then I'm not really being manipulated.

All right.

I roll the dough till the indentations from Claudia's fingers are gone. The whole surface is smooth now.

Claudia says something, then she holds up her index finger and thumb a quarter inch apart.

I roll the dough harder, putting my weight into it, until it's only a quarter inch thick.

Claudia smiles approvingly. Then she takes a knife and slices a length of the dough about two inches wide. She takes that strip and cuts it into triangles, and hands me the knife. Claudia's triangles are all different sizes. So I guess it doesn't matter how I cut mine. I slice the rest of the dough into two-inch-wide strips and cut each strip into triangles.

Claudia puts a frying pan on the stove and fills it a half inch deep with oil. She turns on the burner. And she sings.

I'm the one who sang yesterday. But now Claudia's singing. And I'm sure she's doing it for the same reason she handed me the rolling pin. I want to plug my ears.

But the song is nice. It's got a happy, almost rebellious sound. Maybe I just think that because Claudia's standing taller as she sings it. She punches out the words as though she's fighting someone.

Her brother groans from the living room. I had almost forgotten he was there.

Claudia says something to me. Slowly and clearly.

But I don't understand, of course. I never understand.

I keep my eyes on the oil. The heat makes it rise at the edges of the pan. Tiny bubbles form.

Claudia repeats the words slowly. And then she sings them. And she stops and repeats them slowly. I get it. She wants to teach me the song.

I repeat after her: *"Sebben che siamo donne, paura non abbiamo."* And now it doesn't matter that I don't know what it means, because I like the tune a lot.

Claudia cuts a tiny corner from a dough triangle and drops it in the oil. It puffs up and turns light brown. She scoops it out with a slotted spoon and smiles.

We're singing the song slowly as Claudia drops dough triangles into the oil. I want to drop some in, too. She puts her hand on mine to stop me at first, then she looks at me and takes her hand away. I carefully drop in a triangle. The oil splatters a little, but I don't get burned. Still, I let Claudia put them in after that.

She teaches me more words: *"Abbiam delle belle male lingue, in lega ci mettiamo."*

It's hard to remember so many words when I don't even know what they mean. It's like memorizing a list of numbers. But I've got a good memory, and Claudia's patient. We sing it over and over and over.

And now comes the easy part, and the part I like the best. Claudia throws back her head and sings, *"Ah, li o li o la."* It's wonderful. It really does feel ancient and wild, somehow. Like a wolf howling alone in the woods. I throw back my head and belt it out. I love it.

Daddy would love this song.

Claudia's brother walks through the kitchen and straight to the bathroom. He doesn't shut the door and I can hear him in there. He's gross and horrible.

Claudia calls out something to him.

I hear the bathroom door slam shut.

We sing and fry dough. When we're finished, a big wooden plate the size of a large pizza is piled high with puffed-up, fried triangles. Claudia takes an aluminum cup out of the cupboard. It has a top screwed on, with lots of little holes in it. She gives it to me.

I hold it by the handle. The top is covered with white dust. What's it for?

Claudia gestures that I should turn it over.

So I shake the cup upside down. Powdered sugar sprinkles lightly, making little white spots on the dough. Claudia reaches over and taps the bottom of the cup. A cloud of sugar rises and makes me sneeze. But the dough triangle right under the cup is now completely covered in white. Hitting the bottom is much more efficient than shaking. I hit the bottom and move the can until every triangle of dough is completely white.

Claudia eats one.

So I do, too. It's a doughnut. The best doughnut I've ever tasted. I didn't know that's how you made doughnuts. I laugh.

The father comes in and we eat doughnuts. And the son comes back and eats, too. As though we're one big happy family. It's a lie. I'm eating because I'm hungry and these doughnuts are so good, not because I belong here.

Claudia nudges me, with her nose against my cheek. It breaks my train of thought, it's so surprising. It seems like something a mother animal would do, a cow or a chimp, but not a person. I laugh in spite of myself.

She gives me a mug of hot milk and another little aluminum cup like the one that has confectioners' sugar in it. She pushes a bowl of sugar toward me and sits down with a cup of coffee. The men are drinking coffee, too.

This aluminum cup has brown dust on top of it. I smell. Cocoa. I put sugar in my milk, add cocoa, and stir. Yummy hot chocolate again. And it goes just right with the doughnuts.

Claudia looks at me over her cup and hums.

I'm eating and humming, too. The tune to the song Claudia taught me. I know this isn't how it should be. I know I should be running away. But I can't. Not now. I'm part of something with Claudia. Something that closes us off safe from the men. Just the two of us.

Ah, li o li o la.

(12)

We clean up from breakfast, and Claudia and I brush our teeth side by side. I used to brush my teeth with Mamma. But we haven't done that for a long time. Years. It's funny to do it with Claudia now. It makes me feel like a little kid. Everything in Italy seems to make me feel like a little kid.

Then we give the birds clean water and fill their seed dishes and hang their cages outside the bedroom window again. It makes me happy to see their excited flutterings as we move the cages. They sing like little maniacs now. They probably hang out there twice a day—morning and evening. Before it gets too hot for them. I wonder if they have names.

Claudia disappears down the corridor while I lean out the window. She doesn't seem at all worried that I might try to jump out again. I guess she knows I'm a chicken at heart. Or maybe she's counting on the calming effect of doughnuts and song. Whatever, she's right. I'm not going anywhere.

A huge gray cat comes to sit right under the cages. I wonder if he sat there last night, too. I call to him, "Here, kitty, kitty, kitty."

He looks at me briefly, then sets his eyes, unblinking, on the birds again.

He can't reach them. And the birds don't seem the least nervous at his being there. Still, I say, "Forget it, kitty, you better run off," more just to have someone to talk to.

The cat doesn't look at me. He's totally absorbed in the birds.

There were no animal food dishes around the front or back door. None on the kitchen floor. Who feeds this cat? But I don't have to worry; he looks fat enough. Jersey would love to chase him. Only, I bet this cat could beat Jersey in a fight. There's a kind of intensity to him, like he's ready. Ready and waiting.

Maybe he's hoping one of the cages will just suddenly rust through and birds will drop in his mouth. He's so dumb.

That's what I'm like. I'm just standing here, hoping that someone will come along and save me.

My own thought makes me mad. I can't act like this.

I can't give up. What about Mamma? If someone kid-napped her, she'd never give up on trying to get back to me.

Claudia calls my name as she passes in the corridor, going toward the kitchen. She's dressed now, but her hair is still loose. Her skirt swings and her hair swings. I run after her, determined to do something—I don't know what—just something to try to get free. But before I can think of anything, she scoots me out the back door with the same warning she gave me yesterday—not to go near the road. And in an instant, I have a plan. I take her hand and pull her. After all, I've let her lead me everywhere. It's my turn to lead her.

"*Aspetta.*" Claudia shakes herself free. She rushes inside, but a moment later she's got her shoes on and she's beside me again.

So we're off. I lead the way to the cliff, my eyes on the lookout for snakes. Then I take us beyond where the steps go down to the sea, through the olive grove. And now I lead us into the woods on the other side of the grove. Woods, and more woods, and more woods. The whole way I've been sure I would come upon the trail that Claudia took us on yesterday, the mushroom trail. I was sure I knew where we were. But now I'm lost. Nothing stands out as familiar. I stop and look around.

Claudia takes over. She walks slowly now, hesitantly,

not like yesterday, when she practically marched. But I don't care how long it takes us to get there. So long as we find the trail we were on yesterday, I'll be satisfied. I'm going to follow it today, whether she says no or not. It leads somewhere else, and I've got to go somewhere else.

There's a nice breeze from the sea. It reaches us, even in the woods. I feel like I could walk forever. Those doughnuts gave me energy.

Suddenly we're on the trail. I run ahead. Claudia calls from behind, but I don't care. I won't be a chicken anymore. People walk this trail, and somewhere someone has to help me.

It doesn't take long to get to the wooden bridge. It's sturdy enough, I know that now. But my breath quickens anyway. Claudia's coming behind me. She's not calling out for me to stop—she seems to know that wouldn't work. But she's hurrying. She wants to catch me.

I step onto the bridge carefully. It doesn't sway or anything, but my hands wish there were side rails to hold onto. I walk as fast as I dare.

I'm across, and I run. I don't look back. There's nothing but woods everywhere. I'm running.

Then I remember snakes.

I stop and look back. Claudia's not in sight. So I can

afford to go carefully. I'm lucky I didn't stumble over one when I was running. Today's a lucky day for me. I need a lucky day.

I walk a long time. This must be a forest. Forests are the home of all sorts of wild animals. There are no lions or tigers in Italy. But maybe there are things like cougars. And wild boars, I know there are wild boars, because we saw a metal statue of one, and the businessman with Daddy told us that they're good to eat.

I'm lost in the woods.

I stop and look in every direction nervously.

It's another quarter of an hour before Claudia catches up to me. She takes my hand just as though she expected me to be waiting for her. But she doesn't lead me back the other way. Instead, she keeps going forward on the trail.

In just a few minutes the trail comes out on a clearing. But it's not a meadow, it's a cemetery.

I stop, stunned. I wanted houses and people, not this. No wonder Claudia let me run ahead—she knew there was nothing here.

"*Ecco,*" says Claudia. She uses that word a lot. She throws up her hands and lets them drop by her side. Her gesture seems almost apologetic. She must know how disappointed I am. "*Ecco.*" She walks over to a tombstone and sits on the ground with her back leaning against it. She closes her eyes.

I don't know what else to do, so I walk through the rows of tombstones. They're exactly lined up. At home there's a cemetery right beside the church, and while there's a general sense of rows, it isn't anywhere near as regular as here. Last year in school we studied about Washington, D.C., our nation's capital. I remember a photograph of the Arlington National Cemetery, where the soldiers are buried. The tombstones there were all exactly lined up, like here.

But this isn't a cemetery of soldiers. I walk slowly, looking at all the tombstones. At the top a name is chiseled in big letters, with two dates underneath. Birth and death. And then, in smaller letters, there are words and sometimes more names. The family members. Maybe the children of the dead person. No, these definitely aren't soldiers. These are men and women. Some are even children. And they died at all different times. Many of them have crucifixes on chains dangling over the top of the tombstones.

I move over to the next row and actually step on a snake. I scream and jump away. It flips onto its back, lies still, and gives off a foul odor.

I run smack into Claudia, who came rushing to me.

She takes me by the elbow and pulls me back toward the snake, pointing at it. After a little while, the snake turns back onto its belly and glides away. It was playing dead. And it's the same kind as the other snakes I saw—with two long stripes. Claudia says something. But I don't need to know her words, because I'm sure she's telling me the snake is harmless, and I already know that now. A poisonous snake wouldn't have to play dead; it could fight.

I've been so stupid to be afraid of these snakes.

Now Claudia walks with me from grave to grave. Sometimes she brushes away leaves and dirt, but usually she just looks at them, like I do.

I stop, with Claudia standing right behind me, and read the name on the tombstone she was leaning against before I stepped on the snake. Mazza Antonia Raffaella. I read the dates. This person died a little over a year ago, at ten years old. Now she'd be my age.

My cheeks feel heavy with sadness. There are younger children than this one in the cemetery. There are babies. So I should feel just as sad for them. And I do, really. Still, somehow this is worse. After all, babies get sick a lot, and they can die. But kids my age are strong. What could a person my age die of? I wish I could read the words underneath—maybe they say.

I read the name again. And again. The middle part, Antonia, that part is familiar to me. But I don't know anyone named Antonia.

Prickles go up my neck, up my temples. I remember being in the backseat of the car with the son petting my hair and murmuring.

He said, "Antonia."

(13)

I stare at the words on Antonia's tombstone, searching
for names. If the tombstones of adults have their children's names on them, then maybe the tombstones of
children have their parents' names on them. And there
it is: Grandinetti Claudia Giuseppina. Right smack in
the middle is Claudia. I twirl to face her, my thoughts
scrambling over each other. "Who was Antonia?"

Claudia's looking past me at the tombstone as
though she's in some sort of a trance.

I'm going to take her by the arms and shake her
when I hear a car horn. I turn and run toward the noise
of the motor, across the cemetery and through the trees,
and almost immediately I come out on a bend in the
road.

A small yellow car is going quickly down the hillside. I shout, "Stop," and wave my arms over my head.

The car zooms along, leaving a dust cloud trailing behind. The noise of the motor drowns out my voice, and unless the driver looks in the rearview mirror, he'll never know I'm here. But I'm running as fast as I can anyway, shouting and waving. I fall and crack my chin on the hard dirt. My hands are raw and the scabs on my knees have scraped off. The yellow car honks before the next bend, then disappears around it. And I just bet this is the same dirt road that runs past Claudia's home. It's the only road on this hillside, just one big zigzag, all the way up.

Sometimes I wonder if I have any brains at all. Anyone could have predicted the cemetery would be near the road. You can't carry a coffin along a narrow trail in the woods. When I first got to the cemetery, I should have run ahead to the road. I should have known.

Claudia's walking at the edge of the road toward me.

I stand up. Blood rolls down both shins. I could wipe it off with a leaf. But I'd rather let Claudia see it. If she can manipulate me, she deserves it back.

But now I see her face, her sad face, and the name on the tombstone repeats in my head: Antonia, Antonia, Antonia. When Claudia's close enough to hear me, I say, "Tell me who she was."

Claudia blinks. She leans over to look at my legs, but I take a giant step backward. So she hooks her arm through mine and guides me into the woods again, back to the cemetery.

She heads for the trail in the woods. But I pull her the way I want to go, instead. And she comes easily, as though she's the child and I'm the one guiding her.

I bring Claudia to Antonia's grave, and everything inside me jumbles and swirls. The possibility makes me sick. I don't want to know. But I have to. I have to understand. I point at the tombstone. "Are you her mother? Is that who you are? Did your Antonia die?"

"*Antonia, sì. La mia Antonia.*" Claudia brushes hair off my forehead with the slightest touch of her fingers. Tears make her eyes bright.

I have to be sure. Absolutely sure. I point at the tombstone insistently, then at Claudia. "Mamma?" I ask. "Are you Antonia's mamma?"

"*Sì.*" Her voice is a broken whisper. "*La mia Antonia.*"

I shake my head, wishing it wasn't true. And now the photographs in the bedroom make sense. Antonia didn't put up all those photographs of herself—Claudia put them up after she died. "Oh, Claudia. Oh, no. I'm so sorry your daughter died. I'm sorry."

The tears roll slow and fat down her cheeks.

I'm still shaking my head, but I'm crying, too. "I'm so sorry." Poor, poor Claudia. I want to know how it happened. I want to know everything. But I can't even ask.

She must feel so alone. And—oh, oh no, I think I'm beginning to understand. "Claudia, I'm sorry Antonia died.
But you can't just have me. You can't just take me in her
place." That's it, isn't it? That's it. I wipe my tears as they
fall, and speak as steadily as I can. "Did those men—
your father and brother—did they give me to you like a
present? Is that what happened?"

I think of them driving on that road late at night—
far away from home—finding a little girl alone. They
drove off when I ran to them the first time they stopped.
Maybe because it dawned on them how easy it would
be to take me with no one knowing—maybe they were
horrified at their own thoughts. But then they came
back and they saw Daddy and maybe it was too much—
too much like fate—maybe they thought I was an offering, just waiting there for them.

I take hold of Claudia's forearm. "That's crazy, Claudia. You know that. I'm not an offering. I can't be your
present. I have a mother, too. And that's what I call
her—Mamma—just like Antonia called you."

Claudia leans with one hand on the top of the tombstone, then she lowers herself to the ground. She kisses
the tombstone and works her fingers under her hair on
both sides of her head, so that she's cupping her own
head like a baby. Her body heaves with sobs.

I could go out to the road now. Claudia wouldn't

stop me. I could walk along it until some car came to give me a ride. That would be the practical thing to do. That's what I would have done if this had happened yesterday. But I don't want to leave Claudia crying. I left Daddy—and even though I didn't have a choice, I wish I'd fought. Maybe Claudia's father and brother wouldn't have taken me if I'd fought at the very beginning. No matter, I won't leave Claudia. Not until I'm sure she's okay.

I tug on her arms till she lets go of her hair. She's blinking up at me, her face asking for help, like a little kid. Her hair's a mess now. I try to straighten it with my hands. She gives a hint of a smile. So I go at it with concentration. I separate her hair into three locks and braid it. But when I get to the bottom, I don't know how to hold it together. Then I remember. Of course. I take the pearl hair claw from my back pocket.

Claudia gasps. She touches the hair claw. *"Questo è di Antonia,"* she says.

I can see what the words mean from her face—this was Antonia's. Of course: it has a bird on it. Antonia must have loved birds. That's why her bedroom has all those birds. The photographs and the birds—the bedroom is like a shrine to Antonia. "That's good," I manage to say. "She would have wanted you to have it." And I know that's true. Antonia hid the hair claw in the geode so that it would be safe. She thought it was beautiful, like I do.

I fasten the little claw to Claudia's braid and coax her to her feet. We take the trail back through the woods and across the bridge. Then we leave the trail and wind our way to the olive grove and out the other side.

Claudia wants to go home, but I'm pulling her my way, toward the edge of the cliff. "It's okay," I say. "Come with me. *Vieni*."

"Okay," she whispers. I didn't know she knew that English word. But maybe she said it just because I said the Italian word *vieni*.

I bring her to the steps that lead down to the beach and start on them, but Claudia grabs my arm. She wants me to stop. I yank myself free and climb down.

She calls to me.

"I'll be right back," I say, going as fast as I dare. I have to look carefully, because I didn't count the steps before. But I know the geode was around the middle step somewhere.

There it is. I dig it out of the dirt and hold it against my chest as I climb back up. I hand it to Claudia.

She wipes it off with her skirt and carries it in both hands, as though it's fragile. She walks back to the house that way. And I'm so grateful I found the geode, so grateful I could give it to Claudia.

I follow her inside. The house is empty. I'm not sure how I know that, but I do. Claudia puts the geode on the kitchen table and takes my hand. She brings me to the bathroom and wets a cloth and bends toward my scraped knees.

"I can do it myself." I take the cloth and wash off the dirt and blood.

Claudia hands me a bottle and a puff of cotton and then leaves.

The cap twists off the bottle easily, and the smell is strong. I'm sorry I was so quick to refuse Claudia's help. I just know this stuff is going to sting bad. I pour some on the cotton and dab at my knees. And it does; it stings.

Claudia's back now. She puts something on the shelf beside the sink, then leaves again.

It's my dress, with the big flowers. It's folded on top of my patent-leather shoes. The rip in the skirt is mended with small, even hand stitches. I strip off the shorts and shirt and sneakers and put on my dress and shoes. I go out into the kitchen.

The white car pulls up outside. I know from how the engine coughs before it dies.

Claudia stiffens. She rushes me down the corridor and into Antonia's room. She says something and shuts the door.

I've caught her sense of urgency. My heart beats fast,

and I want to know what's going on, I want to hear what Claudia and her father and brother say to one another. I can't know their words, but just the way they talk to one another might tell me something.

But I can't hear anything over the noise of the birds. Someone brought them in while we were out; the cages stand in the center of the room again. As soon as Claudia pushed me in here, the birds went nuts. They're hopping from perch to floor to perch, knocking into each other and squawking. I talk softly to them, to calm them down, but it doesn't work. Finally, though, they just stop, one after another, until the room is quiet.

They must have thought I was going to hang them outside. After all, probably no one ever comes in this room except to put the birds in or out. I'm sorry I disappointed them.

I listen hard. I press my ear against the door.

Their voices are low and muffled. It's just the brother and Claudia. The old man must not be here. And they're not arguing. My heart falls. I was sure Claudia understood me when she was crying in the cemetery. We know each other now. We have no choice—we're friends. Claudia has to fight. We're friends. We are.

I pace around the room. I'm not certain of anything anymore. But if I don't do something, I'll lose my mind.

I remember the gray cat. I go to the cages and check the bottom rungs, to make sure they're secure. I won't let these birds drop out into the cat's mouth like an offering. No more offerings.

But the cages are strong.

Someone walks into the bathroom and shuts the door loudly.

Claudia slips into the bedroom silently. She puts her fingers to her lips in the hush sign. Then she points at the wall and motions for me to listen.

I put my ear to the wall while she races around the room behind me putting things into a bag. I don't understand what she's doing. She's acting frantic.

The shower turns on in the bathroom.

"He's in the shower," I whisper to Claudia.

Immediately she opens the bedroom door and runs quietly down the corridor. I'm right behind her, through the kitchen, across the living room, out the front door. She gets in the driver's seat of the white car and I jump into the passenger seat. She tosses the bag onto my lap and backs up, turns the car around.

The son comes running out the front door, glistening wet from the shower, a towel wrapped around his waist. He shouts.

But we're already out on the road, and Claudia's

flooring the gas pedal. I watch out the rear window until we turn the bend and I can't see him anymore.

We drive down the hill faster than is safe, but I don't care. Who knows if he's running down the steps, maybe half flying down the steps, planning to jump out in front of us on the road ahead, who knows?

It takes forever to get to the bottom of the hill, and the whole time we don't say anything to each other. We reach the paved road. Claudia looks at me and purses her lips in decision. She squeezes my hand. Then she turns—not in the direction of the hill town. Instead, we're going back the way the father and son brought me from that first day.

I know there are police stations in the hill town. But I don't get scared that Claudia isn't going there. Wherever she's taking me, that's the right thing. I know this now with all my heart.

Claudia sings. It's the song she taught me this morning. I sing with her. We're howling, *"Ah, li o li o la,"* at the top of our lungs. I feel giddy, as though we're in a conspiracy together—we're partners. We drive so long, past the forests and farms and little villages. Up and down hills, always fast. It's got to be an hour. More than an hour. My ears start popping.

We pass the road that leads to the highway. I recognize it because of the big green signs. So we're not going back to Rome.

Claudia drives and drives. There are more cars on the road now. And there are factories. And houses. We're coming into a town. The sign says COSENZA. It's a big town. A city. The upper floors of the buildings have balconies with iron railings. The lower floors have bars over the windows.

Claudia turns several times, looking at every street name. I wonder if she's lost.

And now it dawns on me: Claudia hardly knows this city. That's why we came here. I'm sure it is. This way no one will recognize her. No one will ask her what she's doing with me. No one will try to stop either of us.

We pass a policeman, standing on the sidewalk talking to someone. I look at Claudia, but she doesn't pull over. She turns and drives to a parking lot. She gets out and comes around to my side.

I get out. Claudia reaches into the car and gets the bag that fell off my lap. She makes me hold it.

We walk hand in hand across the street to a train station. There's a train waiting on the tracks. Claudia walks me right up to it. She doesn't even look at the posted schedules. This could be any train, going anyplace. She climbs the steps, pulling me behind her.

"Where are we going?" I say. But then I realize again that she's right. No matter where the train is going, it's going away from here. That's what matters.

She finds an empty seat and sits me in it. Then she kisses me on the forehead and walks to the end of the train car and she's gone.

Here and gone, just like that. Things change in a moment.

This time three days ago, I was walking in Rome with Daddy. Just three days ago. And everything has changed.

I stand up. I can see Claudia out the window, standing on the train platform. She's looking at me. I wave and blow her a kiss. She's crying now. And I'm crying, too. But I know it has to be this way. Otherwise she'd get in trouble. And her brother and father would get in trouble.

They did a terrible thing, taking me like that. And I'll never know for sure why they did it; I'll never be certain of any facts about their lives. But I trust my feelings—and my feelings tell me they did it because they love Claudia. So it doesn't matter what else I know or don't know; I don't want them to go to jail.

Maybe the people around here aren't that strange, after all. Maybe the men just went crazy—temporarily insane—when they saw me by the side of the road. They're not bad.

And Claudia, she's good. I can tell she was a wonderful mother. Poor Claudia.

When Claudia's husband comes home, he won't even know any of this happened.

If he comes home.

Oh, no. I remember him in the photographs in Antonia's room. But only in photographs with a little Antonia. He wasn't in the photographs when Antonia was big, like me.

Maybe they're divorced. Or he died.

Please, please, I'm thinking, oh, please don't let that be true. Please let him come home. Please let Claudia still have him in her life.

I'm waving and waving. So is Claudia.

We stay like that till the train pulls out and she's lost from sight.

I go back to my seat and open the bag. There's the striped cat. And my old underpants and socks, all neat and clean. And the new things they bought for me—the toothbrush and hairbrush and underpants and socks. And there's the nightgown I slept in for the past two nights. Claudia knew I thought it was beautiful. She saw how I touched it.

Antonia won't miss it. She's dead.

People die.

In the very bottom of the bag is a folded newspaper page. It's got the story about Daddy. And me. I clutch it to my throat and look around.

The two seats across the aisle are empty, and one of them has a newspaper on it, folded neatly, but loosely. Someone already read it and left it behind. The front page has a picture of a woman—a woman I know. I put my things on the seat beside me and go over to get the newspaper. Then I sit back down in my seat and look at the woman, who is looking straight into the camera with a tired face, but her eyes are hard with determination. That's Mamma. My mamma. I can hear her talking to herself. She's saying, "Buck up." She's come to get me. Mamma's come.

The train conductor moves through the car, asking for tickets. I smooth the newspapers and put them on the seat beside me so that it's easy to see all the photographs at once. And I pick up the bag that Claudia gave me. I want it in my hands. When the conductor gets to me, I'll point at the newspaper photographs—the old ones and the new one. I'll point at them and tell him who I am. I plan what I'm going to say.

I'm Jackie Holt. These two photographs are me. And that's my mamma. She's come to get me. I have to go to her right away because

. . . I swallow and my eyes brim with tears again . . . *because that's my daddy. He's dead. But I'm alive. I have to tell Mamma I'm alive.*

That's all I'll say. I won't tell anyone where I've been. Because it doesn't matter to anyone, except me and Claudia. I look at the picture of Mamma and whisper, "Buck up. I'm coming."

I curl the edge of the bag in my fists and sing inside my head, *"Ah, li o li o la."*